★BETTER THAN A BULLY★

J.J.'s Friendships & Secrets

BOOK #2

Tina Levine

Illustrated by Ned Levine

www.**readonbooks**.com

Read On Books
www.ReadOnBooks.com

Facebook: www.facebook.com/TinaReadOnBooks/
Instagram: @TinaReadOnBooks
Twitter: @TinaReadOnBooks

PRAISE FOR *BETTER THAN A BULLY: J.J'S FRIENDSHIPS & SECRETS*

Better Than A Bully: J.J.'s Friendships & Secrets fits the middle school dilemma perfectly, giving kids resources without talking down to them.

Dr. Sherryll Kraizer, founder, Coalition for Children
kraizer@safechild.org

J.J.'s Friendships & Secrets, the second title in the *Better Than A Bully* series by Tina Levine, is a delightfully entertaining story that follows the transformation of the title character, J.J., from his unfortunate experiences of being bullied to his learning how to rise above peer cruelty, reach out to helping adults, forge positive friendships, and make a positive difference for his entire school community. *J.J.'s Friendships & Secrets* is a great read for anyone interested in learning how to stand up for themselves, connect with others, and turn a problem situation into an opportunity for leadership and growth.

Signe Whitson, author of
8 Keys to End Bullying: Strategies for Parents & Schools

Better Than A Bully: J.J.'s Friendships & Secrets is a heart-warming story about the transformation of a boy scared to tell adults about being physically bullied at school. In this second book of the series, we hear and see the effects physical bullying has on the bullied, the bystanders, and the bully. Bravo to this upper elementary and middle-grade fiction book engaging readers while sharing strategies on how to handle these challenging situations.

Andrew Pleener, psychiatrist, MD
CEO of Regional Psychiatry
Windermere, Flordia

I am dedicating this book to my children and grandchildren. May they be compassionate and tolerant of others. May they reach their greatest potential and become the best versions of themselves.

Inspiration

"When someone is cruel or acts like a bully, you do not stoop to their level. ***Our motto is, 'When they go low, you go high.'"*** *—Michelle Obama*

{ CHAPTER 1 }

The Pickup

Best day ever! Can't wait to meet up with my buddies. My wish is about to come true.

Last night, after the fifth and sixth-grade spring band and chorus concert, my buddies and I decided to form a band. I've wanted to do this since third grade. Almost all of us play instruments, and we know we can sing, so we made a plan to meet on the school grounds today to try out our voices together.

That was where I was headed now—once we've picked up Ace. Mom agreed to drive him because he still has a cast on his ankle from falling into a hole last week.

Ace has been my friend since kindergarten. Since my name is Justin Jon, Ace nicknamed me "J.J." I like it when he calls me J.J. It means we are buddies! Since I don't have any brothers, I make-believe he's one of mine.

He's always loved coming to my house for home-cooked Chinese food, and I love playing ball in his backyard. There's a huge empty lot behind his house, and no one bothers us there. Sometimes we get kids together for football, baseball, or kickball. I still remember back in third grade when he started hitting baseballs out of the lot, making touchdowns, and tagging people out in kickball. We'd always yell, "You aced that one, Aaron!" That's his real name— Aaron. But because he's so athletic, we call him Ace.

"Justin, Aaron is not outside waiting," Mom said as we pulled up to his house. "Please go ring his bell."

Mom never liked to honk her horn 'cause she didn't want to disturb the neighbors.

I headed up Ace's walk, excited to get to the playground and start singing. Then I heard it: yelling from inside. Through the screen door, I saw Ace's brother, Billy.

"Damn, Aaron, can't you do anything?" Billy screamed. "Just because you have a broken ankle doesn't mean I have to do all your chores. You're so useless!"

I jumped! Something crashed to the floor inside their house. *What was going on in there?* My heart pounded. I didn't want Ace to get hurt again!

"It's all your fault, you little turd!" Billy shouted. "You and that stupid broken ankle! Did you actually slip into a hole on the playground playing tag? How lame is that? Don't forget to look where you're going *today*, dummy. I don't want to have to pick up any slack for you if you go off and break your *other* ankle."

From the door, I watched as Billy laughed and got in Ace's face, poking him in the chest.

Billy made my skin crawl. He was such a bully. I wished someone would put a stop to how he treated Ace, but that seemed like a grown-up problem. *What could I do?*

Suddenly, Billy turned and walked toward me. I stepped back. When I visited Ace, I tried to steer clear of Billy, but it wasn't always easy. With Ace's mom at work or sleeping late some mornings, Billy was sort of in charge. That was a big reason Ace was usually late for school.

Taking a deep breath, I knocked on the door.

"Hey, Aaron, your little friend is here!" Billy called out. "Let yourself in, Little J!"

I hated being called "Little J," but no way did I have the guts to tell Billy that.

Through the screen door, I saw Ace hobbling toward me on his crutches. "I'll be right out, J.J.," he said.

Today, I could tell he was feeling extra quiet from the soft sound of his voice.

I turned around and headed back to the car. Then I heard the screen door slam, with Billy still yelling in the background.

Mom rolled down a window. "Good morning, Aaron," she said. "How are you feeling today?"

"Hi, Mrs. Chang," Ace said quietly. "I'm okay. Thanks for picking me up."

"I'm happy to help you, Aaron," Mom said as Ace slid inside. "How are your mom and dad?"

"They're okay," Ace said. "My dad is in South Africa and won't be home until next Saturday. Mom is probably getting up soon to drive Billy to work so she can use the car to do the food shopping. Then she'll go to the hospital for work."

"Boy, your dad really gets to see the world," my mom said. "I'll bet he comes home with great stories about the places he's been."

Ace shrugged. "Most of the time Dad's too tired from traveling to talk about what he did. But he does take some cool pictures. Mom says she wishes he'd travel less. She doesn't like being home with just Billy and me."

I nodded. I wouldn't want to be alone with Billy, either. I've seen him in action, and it's not just Ace he's mean to. He fights with his mom a lot, too.

"Okay, here we are, guys," Mom said. "Have fun. And Justin, don't forget we have that appointment this afternoon. Call me when you're done. If you're still here when it's time, I'll come get you."

Ace and I walked toward the back of the school. We saw Annie, Tara, and Lexi by the giant concrete barrels at the playground as we got closer.

It's sad to think that just last week, we were still bullying Annie. We used to call her "Carrot Top." Not anymore, though!

She has become a hero in our crowd. After Ace's accident, we found out that she's actually a great leader—not to mention talented and funny. Annie taught us to be calm in a stressful situation. *I wonder where she got those skills?*

It turned out that Annie is really cool. She hasn't had it easy, though. Not only did her dad die in a car accident, but her mom was badly injured. Now Annie has to help at home a lot. The more I learn about her, the cooler I realize she is. Now, we're buddies!

"Hi, Ace!" Annie yelled. "Hi, Justin!"

"Hey, Annie!" I said. "Ready to test out our sound?"

Annie nodded. She, Lexi, Tara, and I ducked into a barrel. Ace leaned against it.

"Okay, Annie, what song should we start with?" Tara asked.

{ CHAPTER 2 }

The Intruder

We sang for a while, testing out different harmonies. It was cool the way our voices echoed in the barrel. Personally, I thought we sounded great! We were about to start a new song when we heard a voice outside the barrel.

"Hey, Ace, what are you up to?"

"Hey, Noah," Ace said.

Noah is in Ms. Ashton's sixth-grade class. He's also in chorus with us. I could tell from the sound of Ace's voice that he wasn't so happy to see him.

"What are you guys up to here with Gimpy?" Noah said.

"Just jamming with some songs," Ace said. "Ignore him, guys. How about we do 'Happy' by Pharrell Williams? We can break up the verses, then sing the chorus together."

"What will you do?" Noah asked.

"I've got my harmonica," Ace said. "I'll play along and sing when I can. I'm mostly here to learn the songs so I can join in later."

"Want to play around with it now?" Annie asked.

"Great idea, Annie," Ace said.

Lexi, Tara, and I yelled out, "Yes!"

"So, Gimpy," Noah said to Ace as we warmed up, "how's your pinhead brother? He is such a jerk. My brother told me your brother, Billy, was suspended from school last week. What's wrong with him, anyway? He's always in trouble."

Billy goes to high school with Noah's brother, Pat, and from what I've heard, they do not get along.

"Why don't you mind your own business, turd?" Ace said.

I scrambled out of the barrel. Ace has a temper, and I didn't want him to do anything he'd regret. Sure enough, Noah and Ace were nose to nose, with Noah poking his finger at Ace's chest.

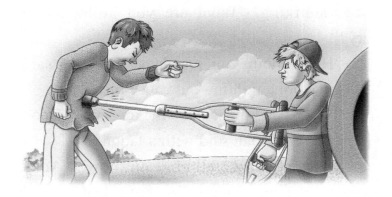

Pow! Ace slammed a crutch into Noah's stomach.

Noah fell to the ground, and Ace toppled over him. I ran over to Ace and helped him up.

"What's going on?" Tara shouted out as she, Lexi, and Annie climbed out of the barrel.

Noah was in pain, but he stood and ran at Ace. I jumped in front of him. I don't know where I found the courage, but when it comes to my buddy Ace being bullied, I guess I just react without thinking. *What else could I have done?*

"Stop right there!" I screamed.

"Oh, good. Here comes the shrimp," Noah said, smirking. "What are you going to do, cry?"

"How about you just leave now," I said. "You've done nothing but cause trouble."

"Who's going to make me? You, pipsqueak?" Noah said with a laugh.

"How about we all chill out now?" Annie said in a firm voice. "We have had enough injuries in the last week. Besides, we came here to sing. This is just a waste of time."

She turned to Noah—and stunned all of us.

"Want to join our band, Noah, instead of fighting?" she asked. "First, though, I think an apology to Aaron would be a good way to clear this all up."

I wondered why she invited Noah to join us after all that fuss. But Annie always seems to know how to calm stressful situations. And having Noah join our band might be good. I knew Ace wouldn't be thrilled about it, but Noah does have a terrific voice and slams it on guitar.

Ace looked at Annie with daggers in his eyes.

Noah glared at Ace, then walked away.

"You okay, Ace?" I asked. "Still want to fool around with some songs?"

"I'm okay," he said. "Noah has always been a pain. He has no right talking about my brother the way he does."

"You're right," Lexi said. "Your brother's business is no one else's.

"Noah does have a great voice, though," Lexi said, fluttering her eyelashes and smiling.

"That he does," Tara admitted with a big smile.

What's wrong with them? I wondered. Why do girls like older guys so much? And why Noah? What makes him so cool? Ugh, girls!

"I can't stand being around him," Ace said. "If you want Noah in the band, I'm out."

"You've got to stay in the band," Annie said. "We don't want someone in the band who will be a problem, so let's just get back to jamming."

We all nodded.

The four of us got back in the barrel and began trying harmonies while Ace listened outside.

"How do we sound out there?" Annie asked him.

"Before that pest came along, you sounded terrific," he said. "Your voices really echoed in there. Maybe next time we can record it."

"YES!" we all shouted.

As we climbed out of the barrel, we saw Noah heading back toward us. All eyes turned to Ace.

"Oh, no. What does Noah want now?" Ace said. "Tell him to leave, or I'm out of here."

"Come on, Ace," Annie said. "Maybe we should hear what he has to say."

Noah drew closer, stopped, and looked intensely at each of us, one at a time.

This was not going to be good. I could feel it in my bones.

"Okay, so… I want to apologize for being a jerk," Noah said. "I need to mind my own business, Aaron. I've been told that I often say what is in my head without thinking before I speak. I'm sorry for calling your brother names. I hope you can forgive me."

I could hardly believe this. Noah *apologizing*? I was shocked, but relieved.

"Justin," Noah said. "I don't think you're a twerp. Last year, you and I worked on a really cool art project together, and our piece is hanging in the school entrance. We had a blast working on it, and you're a talented artist and musician. If anyone's a twerp, it's me for acting the way I did."

I'd never heard Noah talk so politely. I think we were all in a bit of shock.

"This apology is really to all of you," he said. "When I was walking away before, I realized I was jealous. I was standing near Justin after the concert last night. I heard you decide to meet here, and I was upset at not being included. I should have just asked then or called Justin to see if I could be part of your band. It's something I've wanted to do for a while. I figured you wouldn't think I was good enough."

Annie, Lexi, and Tara looked at Ace. His face was a deep shade of pink.

"I hope you will forgive me and let me join the band," Noah said.

Ace looked at us. He shrugged and said, "Whatever they want to do."

"It's really up to Ace and Justin," Annie said. "How about giving us a chance to discuss it, Noah, and we'll get back to you?"

Noah nodded and started to walk away.

"Wait," Ace called. "I've been a bully to other kids at school, too. I bullied Annie for several years. So did Tara, Lexi, and Jus. It took me being in an accident to realize I had been bullying someone I really didn't know very well. It turns out she is a terrific person.

"I'm not perfect, either," Ace continued. "So, I forgive you, Noe... Is it okay if we call you Noe?"

I smiled at Ace. I knew his description of all of us was right. I also understood that a nickname would make Noah feel part of our group. Besides, as my dad always says, "Keep your friends close and your enemies closer." Dad has an expression for everything. Something about this one makes sense.

Annie looked at Ace and said, "What is a Noe?"

Everyone laughed, even Noah. He was a good sport, after all.

"Yep, looks like you're in our band, Noe," Ace said with a smile.

Noah reached out a hand to Ace with a half-smile. Ace reached back and they shook hands.

"Peace?" asked Noah.

"Yeah, Noe, okay," Ace said. "Just leave your comments about my brother out of our rehearsals."

"You got it, Ace," Noah said. "That ends now!

"Hey, have you all decided on the first song?" he said, looking around. "I can learn the words and guitar part."

"Do you know 'Happy'?" Lexi asked with a twinkle in her eye.

"I know of it. But sure, I'll grab the lyrics and listen to it tonight!" Noah said with a smile.

"That's great, Noe!" Lexi said.

Yep, Lexi was thrilled to have Noah in the band.

"I can't wait till we get the instruments into the song," Lexi said. "Where can we rehearse?"

"I'll ask my mom if we can do it at our house," I said. "Dad lets me set up my drums in the garage behind the house, so they don't have to hear me banging away. We can have some privacy. I'll check and get back to all of you."

"Great!" Annie said, giving her trademark Grand Canyon smile. "The only problem for me is that I won't have a ride to J.J.'s house if it is raining. Also, sometimes I have to do stuff at home and need to know ahead of time when you want to practice."

"My mom can probably pick you up, Annie," Tara said. "She's home on Saturdays."

Everyone agreed to practice the song on their instruments before rehearsal next week.

"That should work," said Ace. "I have a travel keyboard I can bring, so long as I have a ride to your house.

"Hey, Annie," he said. "Why don't you be the lead singer since you're not playing an instrument?"

That one got an enthusiastic "Yes!" from the whole group.

"How about a week from today at 2 p.m. for a couple of hours?" I said. "Let's all check with our parents and see if we can set this up."

"So, Gimpy, are you coming next week, too?" Noe asked with a smile.

"Yep, I'll be there," Ace said.

This time, Ace knew that Noah was just kidding around.

"You know," Annie said, "teasing is cool if it's for fun. I always tell friends something is up with me if I don't tease you a little. My mom and dad always used to tease each other. I could tell by the sound of their voices they were joking around. Let's promise each other not to be mean."

Noah nodded. "I promise."

Just then, my phone buzzed in my pocket.

"Ugh, I gotta go," I said. "My mom made an eye doctor appointment for me. She's headed here now. See you all on Monday. I'll let you know if we can practice at my house next Saturday."

As Ace and I walked up to meet my mom, I wondered if this was all going to work out with Noah. His apology *did* seem genuine. All in all, I had a feeling we were gonna make some great music together.

CHAPTER 3

Four Eyes

UGH! Over the weekend, I found out I have a weak muscle in one of my eyes and I'm farsighted, so now I have to wear glasses all day. *How unfair is that!*

"Mom, do I *really* have to wear these glasses all day at school?" I whined as I entered the kitchen for breakfast.

"Good morning to you, too, Justin," Mom said. "I know you're not happy about this, but the eye doctor gave you strict instructions. Dad wears glasses all day and he's fine. You will get accustomed to them, too. Now eat your breakfast."

I sat down but barely ate. Mostly I just pushed food around the plate. Then I went back to my room to get dressed. I looked in the mirror without my glasses while combing my hair.

Okay, so it's a bit blurry.

Sighing, I put on the glasses and looked again. There I was, clear as day. My eyes look magnified. UGH! It was bad enough that I was short for my age, now this! I could almost hear the insults. *Shorty with four eyes.*

Maybe I could make-believe I was sick and not have to go today. It was worth a try.

I walked downstairs, bent over with my head low.

"I feel awful, Mom," I said. "My stomach is killing me. I just want to go back to bed."

"Let me feel your head," she said. "You don't feel warm. Did you use the bathroom this morning?"

"Yeah, I did. But I don't feel okay. My stomach keeps getting tight," I said softly.

"Hmm," Mom said. "Okay, go back upstairs, but don't change your clothes. I'll have Dad come up and look at you."

I went back to my room to lie down. A few minutes later, Dad came in.

"Hey, buddy, Mom tells me you're not feeling well," he said. "What's going on?"

"I have a stomachache, Dad. I need to stay home," I muttered.

I looked up at my dad, hopeful he'd buy it, but I doubted he would. My dad happens to be a pediatrician—and a good one, at that.

"I can take your temperature and check out your throat," he said. "Did you go to the bathroom this morning? Or is there something bothering you that you're not telling me?"

Yup, when you have a dad who is a pediatrician, there's no faking anything. As soon as I looked at him, tears welled up in my eyes.

"I just can't go to school wearing these glasses all day," I sobbed.

"I understand that you're not comfortable, son," Dad said. "But you *are* going to school. I had to wear glasses the whole time I was growing up, and I still do. Without them, I would not have been able to become a doctor to help children. Now *that* would have been a shame.

"You have so many talents that glasses will help with," he continued. "How will you draw those amazing comics and whimsical characters? You love to read. How will you understand the comics you love so much? Don't you have to read the words for songs in chorus and the music for the band?"

Dad paused and then added, "Think of it this way… four eyes are better than two. Do the math!"

Dad always cracks jokes—corny ones! I thought about it for a moment and held back my laugh. I wasn't in the mood for a joke, but it *was* sort of funny.

"You're right, Dad," I whispered. "I never thought of it that way." Then I smiled and hugged him.

***

"See you later!" I yelled out to my parents as I ran out to the door to meet up with Tara.

She was waiting outside her house. I knew Tara would be nice about my glasses, but I was still nervous. She would be the first friend to see them.

"Hey, Justin, what took you so long?" Tara said. "We're gonna be late. You okay?"

"Yeah, thought I had a stomachache this morning. Let's go."

Tara nodded. "Glad you're feeling better," she said. "If we walk fast, we can get there on time. Cool glasses, by the way."

I smiled. "Thanks, T!"

Even though I knew Tara wouldn't say anything mean, it was nice to get her compliment.

I wonder what the other kids at school will say. I hope they're as cool about my glasses as Tara!

***

At school, the line of kids was already moving inside. Tara and I followed the others. We all waited for our teacher outside the classroom.

"Hey, Justin, when did you get those glasses?" Brittney shouted from the middle of the line.

I looked up, surprised to hear *her* talking to *me*. I've liked Brittney since second grade, but I didn't think she even knew my *name*. I froze for a second. My heart pounded and my thoughts raced.

Oh my god, Brittney is actually talking to me! Talk back. Say something!

"I got them over the weekend, because I was seeing stuff a bit blurry," I finally managed.

"Well, they're cool," Brittney said. "And they'll probably help you. My older sister wears glasses, and she always talks about how much better she can see with them. Plus, you look smarter."

Then there was silence. I could actually hear my heart pounding in my chest. I liked Brittney, but my brain always seemed to freeze whenever I had a chance to talk to her.

I was thankful Mrs. Lerner came along and opened the classroom door. We headed for our assigned desks.

I put away my jacket and walked to the front of the room with my head low to give Mrs. Lerner a note about my glasses. She looked up and smiled. "Good, Justin," she said softly. "I know this will help you a lot with all of your subjects."

On the way back to my seat, Annie said, "Sharp-looking glasses, Justin."

I smiled. "Thanks, Annie."

She always had something good to say. But that's just Annie being Annie.

The morning went by fast, and I had to admit, the glasses helped me get through all of the classwork more quickly. Without squinting, I could read the assignments more easily, which meant I had more free time to draw before lunch and recess.

Mrs. Lerner lets us have free time if we finish our work early, so I pulled out my drawing pad. Some of the kids who sat near me in the class started passing around my drawings. It made me feel good to hear classmates laughing about the humor in my cartoons or complimenting me on how I drew them.

***

The bell rang for lunch. I was a little nervous about going to the lunchroom with my glasses on, but I hadn't brought lunch from home, so I didn't have a choice.

I was first in line with my class, but somehow I ended up behind a group of older kids. I lowered my head, hoping none of them would notice my glasses. But it was no use.

Hey Justin, when did you get **four eyes** instead of two?

A sixth-grade boy named Eric, standing right in front of me, said it loud enough for everyone to hear.

"You know, you're only supposed to have two eyes," Eric said. "Know who has more than two eyes? Bugs! You a bug?"

Suddenly, he kicked me. I yelped in pain.

All the sixth graders around him laughed, too.

I was used to Eric calling me mean names in the past, but the kick was a new low.

I limped away, embarrassed. I knew if I stayed, I'd probably cry, which would just get a teacher's attention. I didn't need any more attention.

Even though everyone knew Eric bullied kids, his kick hurt me inside and out. I decided to skip lunch and head to the nurse for some ice.

My leg didn't hurt that bad, but I needed an escape from being embarrassed in front of the other kids, and Miss Lolly's office was a safe place to chill out.

From his spot in the lunch line, Ace saw me limping away and followed on his crutches.

"You okay, J.J.?" he said. "What happened, and where are you going?"

"I bumped into something, Ace. I'm fine," I insisted. "I just need some space. I'll hang out with the nurse until lunch is over. I'm not hungry, anyway."

Ace nodded. "Give me your lunch money. I'll have someone bring you something to eat," he said. "I'll come by after recess and walk back to class with you."

I smiled. Ace knows when to give me space, but I also knew we would talk about it later.

In the nurse's office, Miss Lolly looked up as I hobbled into the room.

"What happened, Justin?" she asked.

"Oh, I just tripped as I was getting into the lunch line," I said.

Miss Lolly looked at my leg. Then she had me lie down and put ice on it.

I felt weird lying to Miss Lolly. She was always kind whenever I came to her office. But I didn't want to say anything about Eric. That would only cause other kids to think I was a wimp or a tattletale.

Ace was good to his word, and a few minutes later Annie came by with a sandwich for me.

I thanked her and bit into my sandwich. Any other day it would have been delicious, but today it tasted like cardboard.

**

By the end of recess, my leg felt better. Outside the nurse's office, Ace was waiting for me.

"Hey, J.J., you okay?" he asked as we walked in the hallway. "Some kids told me what happened with you and that kid Eric. I'll tell you, when I am healed from this dumb injury, I'm gonna take care of Eric after school for doing this to you!"

"No, don't bother with that, Ace," I said. "I have to work this out myself. He'll only think I am more of a loser if you try to fight for me."

Ace and I walked into class, and I went to my seat. Everyone stared at me, and I think I blushed, but I tried to ignore them. Now I was short, four eyes, with a limp. *Can things get any worse today?*

"Hey, Justin. You okay?" Brittney asked.

"I'm good," I whispered. *Does she actually care about me?*

{ CHAPTER 4 }

Creative Relief

"Okay, everyone, we have art this period," Mrs. Lerner announced. "Please line up near the door."

Yeah! My favorite subject! I love art. It's the one place where I can shine and not think about the stress of being short with bug-eyed glasses—except in chorus and when I play the drums, of course.

In art, we can sit anywhere, which is cool. I grabbed a spot next to Brittney. *Maybe I'd get to talk to her again.*

35

"Settle down, now!" Mrs. Randle said. "Today we are going to start a new unit: designing an ad for a product. You will work in teams of four or five. Each person will have a job. First, let's look at some samples of how real products are presented online by advertising teams."

On the smartboard, Mrs. Randle showed us ads we'd all seen on social media and TV. Then she handed out sheets of information about the roles we could play in our teams.

When it was time to form groups, she came to my table first.

"Okay, at this table we'll have Justin, Lexi, Annie, Aaron, and..." Mrs. Randle paused to look for a fifth member.

Please say Brittney. Brittney is a really great designer. I remembered how beautifully she designed her book report covers. Plus, it would give me a reason to talk to her!

"...Brittney," Mrs. Randle finished. "The five of you, get together and decide who will take each role."

That was easy for our group. Everyone knew I would be the artist and Brittney the designer. Lexi loved researching on the internet, so she could create a PowerPoint. Annie would organize us and run a budget because of her terrific math skills. We decided Ace would be our client, which was easy-peasy for him. He always likes being the boss.

"Okay, teams," Mrs. Randle said. "By next class, I want each of you to come up with a product to advertise and a rough draft for your ad."

When the bell rang, Annie whispered, "Hey, guys, why don't we have a quick team meeting out front this afternoon before we go home?"

The rest of us nodded. That sounded good to us.

***

After school, I went to the front of the building. Ace, Annie, and Lexi were waiting outside.

I couldn't wait for Brittney to show up! Aside from her beautiful smile and long brown hair, she has a sweet personality.

There are probably a ton of guys in my grade who like her. But I get to be in a group with her! The question is, will she ever like me too?

"As the CEO of my video game company, I would like a new ad created for my favorite game, Spider-Man," Ace sang out, smiling.

I grinned back. It was just like Ace to jump into a role without hesitation.

Just then, Brittney joined us. *Yes!*

"Sorry it took me so long," Brittney said. "I had to stop off to get some homework for a friend."

"That's okay," Annie said, "but I do have to get home in case my mom needs me. Do you all want to come to my house to brainstorm?"

We looked at each other and nodded. Then everyone called home to let their parents know we were going to Annie's.

"Uh, my mom is here to pick me up," Lexi said. "We have a quick errand to run. She can drop me off when we are done, though.

"Ace, you want a ride, so you don't have to walk that far?" Lexi said.

"That sounds great, Lexi. Thanks!" Ace said. "Then I just need to figure out how to get home later!"

"I'm sure mom will give you all rides back to your houses when she picks me up," I said. "You know my mom. She loves to help!"

We waved goodbye, and then Annie, Brittney, and I headed to Annie's house. I was really excited to walk next to Brit. That was my nickname for her. I felt shy about starting a conversation.

Thankfully, Brittney spoke up. "Hey, Jus, what happened to you at lunch? We didn't see you at recess, either."

She called me Jus! And she was looking for me!

Shaking my head, I said, "I'd rather not make a whole thing of it, Brit. Eric from sixth grade was just being his jerky self, same as always."

Brittney smiled. I think she liked that I called her Brit.

"I understand how you feel," she said.

"By the way, J.J., I really think you look SPEC-TAC-U-LAR with your glasses," Annie said with a smile that made her freckles spread out across her face. "Don't let anyone else tell you otherwise."

I smiled, and from the corner of my eye, I think I saw Brit smile, too. At least, I hoped so.

At Annie's house, Brittney went inside to use the bathroom. Annie and I waited outside for Lexi and Ace to arrive.

"I know you don't want to talk about what happened at lunch today, but I saw all of it," Annie said. "I just want to make a suggestion. Think about telling your mom and dad. They may have good ideas to help you with Eric. Maybe even ideas that won't make a big fuss around the school. If you let the bullying go on without a plan, you will be at his mercy every time."

It was quiet for a moment. I felt a little uncomfortable talking about all of it.

"No one has physically bullied me, only with words," she continued. "But when I've been called names or socially excluded, I used humor to distract the bullies. I have no time to be bothered with it or to show people how I feel.

It only makes them do it more. But talking to someone does help sometimes."

Annie put her hand on my shoulder, letting me know she would always be there for me. Like I said, that's just Annie.

Just then, a car pulled up. Lexi got out, and I helped Ace out with his crutches.

"Hey, Mom, we're here!" Annie sang out as she opened the door to her house.

"In the living room, Annie," her mom called back.

Annie's mom wheeled herself into the hallway and smiled.

"Well, I met Brittney a few minutes ago; now it's nice to meet all of you," she said. "You can use the living room to hang out and work on your project."

"Thanks, Mom," Annie said. "After I finish here with my art team, I'll help you cook dinner."

We all looked at each other in awe that Annie was so helpful to her mom. Making dinner certainly wasn't a task any one of us would be doing when we got home.

"Okay," Annie said to everyone as we settled in. "So what should we advertise?"

"Let's do a video game, either a new Spider-Man, Minecraft, or Fortnite: Battle," Ace said.

"I can research the video game that would be most popular with our grade," Lexi said. "Maybe we can even do a survey and get opinions."

I took out a pad and started sketching an idea for a Spider-Man ad. I began with some buildings in New York City and then a cool dive by Spider-Man, swinging off his web onto the top of the Empire State Building.

Everyone gathered around. That felt terrific. Brit even sat in the chair next to me. *Heaven!*

"Hey Jus, how about a bold, chiseled typeface for the title?" Brittney said. On her phone, she showed the word ***SPIDER-MAN*** in all capital letters.

"That looks rad!" Ace said.

"Yeah, Brit, love that choice!" I said.

Then I turned the page and started to draw space gladiators for the Fortnite ad.

In the meantime, Brittney found a cool typeface for the title. "How do you think this looks?" she said, showing the bold word **FORTNITE.**

"I'll create a survey," Lexi said. "During recess tomorrow, I'll walk around and ask which game the fifth graders like most."

"I think we have some great ideas," Annie said. "Why don't we share them by email? Ace, let me know the budget. Then when we get the results of Lexi's survey, we can decide which ideas to use for our ad campaign."

"Justin and Brittney, when all is decided, send me your final sketches for our presentation," Lexi said. "I'll create a file for our presentation."

"Sounds great," Annie said. "I've got some time before I have to start dinner. Let's hang out in front until you all have to go home."

"This is going to be a cool project!" Brit said. "I can't wait to get started."

Outside, I realized that spending an afternoon on our art project helped me forget about the Eric incident for a little while. Time spent with good friends, Brittney sitting next to me, and being creative—the best!

"Hey, does anyone want to play tag early tonight?" I asked. "It's staying light out longer now. Evie, who lives next door to me, invited me, Tara, and Lexi to play a neighborhood game. She doesn't mind when a few extra peeps show up. That just makes the game more fun. Ace, Annie, Brit, see if you can join us."

"Hmm, not sure I can get there," Annie said. "I'll see if I can get a ride from my uncle."

Ace pointed at his leg. "Not sure I'm up for a game, but I'll keep it in mind."

Just then, my mom drove up. When I asked if she'd give everyone a ride home, she said yes. She's the best mom! Then I remembered what

Annie suggested. Should I bring up the topic of Eric this evening with my parents?

If I tell them, I wonder what they will say. Don't want a whole fuss made about it, 'cause I know things would only get worse for me with Eric.

CHAPTER 5

Hard to Believe

As we climbed into Mom's car, I hoped my parents would let me play tag after dinner.

"Can you believe how much Annie helps her mom?" Lexi asked. "I feel so bad that I used to make fun of her. I really saw Annie differently after the spring concert. She has such a beautiful voice. I always thought she was nerdy because of how she dressed, but now I know better. She is so sweet, and smart, too."

"It's important not to judge people, especially if you don't know them," my mom said. "You never know the truth of what's going on at home."

I can't be sure, but I could have sworn I saw Mom look at Ace as she said that last bit. Yeah, my mom definitely knows Aaron is getting bullied at home.

After Mom dropped off the last of my friends, she turned to me.

"I got a call from the nurse today," she said. "Miss Lolly said you tripped at lunch. Are you okay?"

How much do I tell her? How do I get out of this?

"I'm fine, Mom," I said. "Thanks for giving rides to my friends. You're the best! I'm going to get all my homework done as soon as we get home."

I meant every word of that compliment, but I also hoped it would distract her.

"Okay," Mom said. "But no dillydallying on the computer. I want your homework finished before dinner."

"I will get it done. I promise, Mom," I replied.

***

After homework, I went to the kitchen for dinner. We said a prayer before eating, and I wondered if I should bring up what had happened at school. I heard Annie in my ear. *They may have good ideas to help you with Eric.*

Maybe. But I really can't handle a lecture tonight.

"So, Dad, any cool stories about work today?" I asked.

"No, but Mom tells me the school nurse called home," he said.

Uh-oh. Now they've got me cornered!

"Oh, it was nothing," I said, shrugging it off.

"It must have been something for you to stay there the whole lunch period and recess, Justin," Mom said firmly.

"Be honest, Justin!" Dad said. "Tell us why you didn't have lunch or recess today. Miss Lolly told Mom you injured your leg and needed to rest. Is that true?"

"Um, yeah, I sort of tripped while I was on the lunch line. I'm good."

"Okay, Justin, if that's all, then fine. But if there is anything else you want to tell us, you know we're here for you." Mom smiled.

I paused, then said, "Okay, fine. That's not the whole truth."

Lying to them would only create more problems for me. I also worried that they could cancel my band rehearsal on Saturday if I didn't tell them what really happened.

"A sixth-grade boy on the lunch line kicked me and called me Bug Eyes," I said. "It hurt. I was able to walk, but I felt embarrassed. I just wanted to get away from him. Miss Lolly's office seemed to be the best place. I really don't feel like talking about it anymore. Please. For now, that's all I'd like to say. Please respect my feelings. I'm handling it on my own. If I decide I want to talk about it more, I will come and tell you."

"Okay, Justin, just so long as you know you *can* talk to us," Mom said.

"I do know," I said. "I just don't want to make a whole fuss about it. That would only make it worse. Please trust me."

Dad gave Mom his "dad" look, which meant, *Let's give him some space.* He always seems to know when to back off. Mom, on the other hand, is very protective.

I wonder if all moms are like that, or just mine?

"That's fine," Dad said. "For now, just try to avoid that boy. If it happens again, we will need to discuss the situation further."

I knew neither one was completely satisfied with my answer, but I was glad they were going to let me handle it on my own. Besides, I wanted to play outside after dinner and not have any intense discussions. Seeing my friends for a little while was definitely what I needed to forget about Eric.

"Guess what?" I said, trying to change the subject. "I'm working on a really cool art project with some kids in my class. We have to create an ad for a product. That's why we went to Annie's house today, because we're all on a team."

"That's great, Justin," Dad said. "Can you tell us more about the project?"

***

"Some of my friends are meeting at Evie's house next door to play tag in our backyards," I said after I finished eating. "May I please be excused to join them?"

"Okay, Justin," Mom said. "But not for more than an hour."

"Yes!" I shouted and raced out the door.

At Evie's house, Lexi, Brittney, and a girl named Ginny were standing in a circle. I was so happy to see Brittney! I did wonder why Ginny was there, though. Evie had never invited her to a game of tag before.

Ginny was in fifth grade, too, but not in my classes. The girls in my class always talked about how she had the most beautiful platinum blond hair. It did seem nice. And long! All the way down to her waist! But I liked Brit's hair more.

Just then, a car pulled up with Tara and Annie. I smiled and waved, glad that Annie was getting a chance to play with us this time. Tara's mom must have gone to pick her up.

A minute later, another car drove up and Ace climbed out with his crutches. "Thanks, Mom," he said.

"Yeah, yeah, I know," Ace said. "How am I going to play tag with crutches?"

He laughed. "Easy, I'll be the referee, making sure no one cheats."

Boy, was I happy to see him. I didn't want to be the only boy in the group.

"Okay," Evie said. "Let's all get into a big circle." Evie was in sixth grade, so she was automatically in charge.

We all gathered around. Evie stood next to Tara, then came Lexi, Brittney, me, Ginny, Annie, and Ace. I made sure to stand next to Brit. Ace looked across the circle at me. I could tell he would have preferred standing near me, instead of between girls.

Man, it feels good to be out here. Outside, playing with friends, homework is done, no Eric! Aaahhh, free!

"Let's play 'Telephone' before we play tag," Evie said. "That game is hilarious! Remember, everyone close your eyes... no peeking! I will whisper a secret message to Tara. She'll whisper it to Lexi, then Lexi to Brittney, and so on. Ace, you're last. If you can repeat the message perfectly, you'll get to pick the first person to be 'it' in tag."

I remembered this game from a birthday party, and the message did become pretty funny by the end of the circle.

The secret went around in whispers. Then Brittney repeated it to me.

"Let's play a trick on Ginny," she said in a low voice.

While Brittney was whispering, I heard footsteps behind me. I squinted to see what was going on and wondered whether I'd heard the message correctly. I saw Evie walking around the circle with scissors in her hand. She was just behind Ginny.

Suddenly, Evie cut a piece of Ginny's long blond hair with the scissors!

Ginny screamed! Evie raced off toward her house as I stood there in shock. It had happened so fast that I could hardly believe what I had seen!

Everyone else opened their eyes and saw Ginny crying and running off to her house. It was too late. Her hair was cut, even before I could yell out!

Behind us, Evie ran into her house and slammed the door. We all stood glued to the grass, silent, waiting to see if Evie would come back out, or if her parents would come to see what all the screaming was about.

Finally, I blurted out, "I saw everything!"

They all looked at me.

"What did you see?" Tara asked. "Why was Ginny crying?"

"Evie cut Ginny's hair!" I said frantically.

"Oh no!" Tara said. "Evie has always been jealous of Ginny's hair. She told me that a few weeks ago when we were hanging out together after dinner. But to cut it off? Is that her hair on the ground? Wow! It's a pretty long piece."

Is that why she did it? Because she was jealous?

"Maybe we should leave," Lexi said. "I don't want anyone to think I participated."

"Me neither," said Brittney.

"That was awful. Someone should say something," Annie said.

"Well, I *am* the one who saw Evie do it!" I said. "Should I tell her mom?"

"Uh, I think Ginny's mom should do that," Brittney said. "My mom would want me to go straight home."

Lexi and Brittney quickly walked up the block together.

"I'll call my mom," Tara said. "She can drive Ace and Annie home. J.J., do you want someone to stay with you if you're going to tell Evie's mom what happened?"

"No, since I saw it, I should be the one to share what happened," I said. "You guys go home. I'll head back to my house and think about it. See you tomorrow."

As my friends walked away, I looked at Evie's house. *Someone has to tell someone what happened, RIGHT?*

Before I could decide, I saw Ginny and her mom walking swiftly toward Evie's home. I watched them from my front stoop. My heart pounded. Ginny's mom yelled at Evie's mom, Mrs. Frank, but I couldn't make out the details.

Except, then Evie's mom yelled, "My daughter would never do something like that. Don't you accuse my daughter! How do you know no one else in the group did it?"

I didn't understand the rest, but Ginny was still crying. Then she and her mom headed back to their house.

I felt a knot in my stomach. Something moved me off the stoop and up the walkway to Evie's house. I could not stand by and watch Ginny get bullied without the truth being told. But I was nervous. Then I felt my hand knocking on Evie's front door. From behind the door, I heard screaming, then silence. Suddenly, the door opened. It was Evie's mother, a bit red in the face.

"Mrs. Frank, I have to tell you, I saw everything," I said. "Evie *did* cut Ginny's hair, and that is the truth."

Evie's mother glared at me and said, "Don't be such a tattletale, Justin. Mind your business and just go home." Then she slammed the door.

My insides felt like a flash of lightning had gone right through them. I didn't know what to do!

Should I tell Mom and Dad what happened? Evie didn't do anything to me, but I do have to live on this block with her. If I tell my parents, they might not let me play with kids on the block. Maybe I'll just be more cautious if Evie is in an outside game. Besides, she probably knows I told on her, so I'll probably be on her blacklist for a while. Yeah, I can handle this myself.

Still horrified by what I had witnessed, I went home. Now I knew how Ace felt hearing that Eric had bullied me at school and not saying anything because I asked him not to. But I *had* spoken up, even if it hadn't done any good. I felt right about doing that, anyway.

***

Once inside my house, I raced past my parents and upstairs to shower, brush my teeth, and get into bed early, hoping they would not bring up the school incident again. I hopped into bed, covered myself with a blanket, and closed my eyes.

"Okay, Jus, what is going on?" my dad said, turning on the bedroom light.

I peeked out of my covers, and there he was.

"You came in from outside and raced up here without even a good night to us," he said.

"I'm fine," I said, "just tired. Can we talk another time?"

"You know, Justin, I was bullied in school when I was your age," he said. "It was a boy named Charlie. He always called me 'Squint.' Only it wasn't about glasses or about my size. It was because our family comes from China."

Weird, no one has ever called me that name. Shorty, sure. Shrimp? Absolutely! But no one even cares that I'm Chinese American.

"That's weird, Dad," I said. "Why would anyone bother you about being Chinese American?"

Dad shrugged. "Most everyone where I went to school was Caucasian," Dad told me. "It just made me different."

"How were you bullied?" I asked.

"That, I'll tell you another time," he said. "It's getting late. I just want you to know that I understand. I was afraid to tell anyone, too. I knew if I did, it would get worse with the bully outside of school. You see, he lived not too far from our apartment. I had to walk past his house to get home."

"That's exactly what I'm afraid of, Dad," I said. "If I tell on him, he might get me when I'm riding my bike home.

"What did your parents tell you to do about the bullying?" I asked.

"Let's talk about it tomorrow, Jus," he said. "You need to get some rest for school. Just steer clear of Eric."

He bent down and kissed my forehead. "See you tomorrow after school, Jus," he said.

Somehow, Dad always knew how to calm me down. But after he left, I couldn't stop thinking about what he told me.

I wonder how Dad was bullied, and how he's planning to help me.

{ CHAPTER 6 }

Slammed

I met Tara at her door, and the two of us started walking to school.

"Can you believe what happened last night?" she asked.

"It was awful. I still can't believe it," I said.

"Poor Ginny, she had no idea what was going to happen in that game," Tara said. "I wonder if she'll even come to school today."

Suddenly, we heard running steps behind us. It was Lexi crossing the street.

"Hey, guys, wait up!" she called out.

"That was awful last night with Ginny and Evie," Lexi said.

Turning to me, she said, "Did you tell your parents about it?"

I shook my head. "No. I didn't say anything. I think I was in shock."

"I mentioned it to my mom," Tara said. "I'm not allowed to play over there anymore—which is fine by me. That was so mean of Evie to do to Ginny. We do *not* need to hang out with her!"

"Definitely!" Lexi and I strongly agreed.

***

When we got to school, I saw Ace being dropped off by his brother, Billy. He joined us on our line. The sixth graders were next to us, and I looked around to be sure I was nowhere near Eric. Then I saw him in the middle of the sixth-grade line.

"Hey, there's the Shrimp with four eyes," I heard Eric say to his friends.

Lexi had moved up to the front of our fifth-grade line, so I hurried behind her. It's like my dad was in my head: *Just steer clear of Eric.*

We all held places for each other in line, so I figured no one would know I was trying to avoid Eric by joining Lexi. I waved to Ace to join us up front and held the door for him to get inside.

"So, J.J., how are you doing today?" Ace asked. "You cool after yesterday with Eric?"

"Yeah, I'm good," I said. "Just planning on steering clear of Eric as often as I can."

"Hey, J.J.," I heard Annie call out. "Wait for me!

"You okay now, from yesterday at lunch?" she asked me.

I nodded yes while walking into our classroom.

"Hey, J.," Brittney said as I passed her desk.

I liked that she called me "J." I sensed she liked me, so I think my face turned a little pink.

***

"Settle down, now!" Mrs. Lerner said. "Your morning work is listed on the whiteboard. Please get started."

We took out our work folders. My classwork was definitely easier now because I could see so well. If I got this work out of the way, I might have a chance to do some group work later. Maybe I'd even get to work with Brittney on our art project.

"Justin, please come to my desk," Mrs. Lerner said.

Am I in trouble? Why does she need me now? This is so unfair. Now I have to walk to the front of the room, and everyone can see me in my glasses.

"Sit down next to me, Justin," she said softly. "I would like to go over some of your work from yesterday."

I saw that everyone else was busy, so the pressure was off.

"By the way, Justin, you look handsome in your new eyeglasses," she said. "Are they helping you see your work better?"

"Yes, I have to admit they *do* help," I said. "I think I'm getting through my work more quickly."

"That's why I called you up here, Justin," she said. "Your morning work was terrific yesterday, but the afternoon work seemed rushed, not like you. I know you went to the nurse. She reported to me that you hobbled into her office. Do you want to talk with me about it?"

"No, it was just something that happened on the lunch line," I said softly. "I'm good today."

"Okay, Justin," she said. "Please let me know if you want to discuss it with me or Mrs. Pennick, the social worker."

"It was just someone annoying," I said respectfully. "I will deal with it. If I need your help, I'll let you know."

"I hear that you want to deal with this matter on your own," Mrs. Lerner said. "But if it happens again, the school will need to get involved."

I nodded. "Can I go back now and do my work?" I asked.

"Of course you can," she said. "Remember, I am here for you."

***

The morning passed quickly, but at lunch, my stomach tightened. I had to be on the lookout for Eric. But I'd brought my lunch today, so at least I got to skip the lunch line!

I went over to our favorite table and pulled out my lunch bag. In two seconds, it was passed down the table. Everyone wanted to see what my dad drew on my paper bag. Today, it was Batman and Robin flying through the sky in the Batmobile.

Then, the commotion of trading lunches began. Ace traded his apple for Lexi's home-made doughnut. Tara exchanged half of her turkey sandwich for Brittney's chicken nuggets. And I just wanted my lunch bag back. I had to admit I was proud of my dad's talent. Everyone made such a fuss about his drawings. *I wish I could be half as good an artist as him.*

Annie sat next to me. "So, Justin, all ready for our rehearsal on Saturday?" she asked.

"Yes, we're all set for my house at 2 p.m.," I said.

"I was wondering if you could still have it, especially with what happened last night to Ginny," Annie said. "Did you tell your parents about it?"

"No, and I don't plan to, Annie," I said.

"Did you get a chance to talk with your parents about Eric?" she whispered.

"A little, but I am keeping that real quiet for now," I said.

"I get it," she said. "Well, I'll definitely be staying away from Evie."

"Me too," I agreed.

Annie was silent for a second. Then she yelled out, "Hey, Jus! I have a good one," so everyone around us could hear her.

"What is black, white, green, and bumpy?"

"Um, I know it's not a newspaper," I said.

"Nope. It's a pickle wearing a tuxedo!" she said with a laugh.

Everyone at the table laughed. Then they all started telling jokes. Leave it to Annie to change a serious conversation into a fun time!

By the end of lunch, I'd forgotten all about Evie and Eric.

***

We headed for the back doors of the school. Once outside, everyone ran in different directions. Recess was freedom!

My friends liked to play kickball, so most of them ran toward the field. Annie and Tara chose teams. Ace tossed a coin to see who would kick first.

Annie yelled out, "Heads!"

"Bad luck," Ace said. "It's tails."

"That's okay," Annie said. "I love fielding!"

Tara was first up. Annie rolled the ball, and Tara slammed it past the infielders. In the outfield, I ran back and back and back to catch the ball.

Bang! Something slammed my head from behind, and I dropped to the ground.

"Hey there, Four Eyes!" a voice said from just above me. "Watch where you're going!"

I rolled over and sat up. I didn't need to look. It was Eric.

My nose bled, and my glasses were bent and broken. I put my head back to try to stop the bleeding. My head throbbed and I felt dizzy.

"Sorry, I must have bumped into you," I said, looking up at him.

"That's a dangerous sport for a little man like you, Four Eyes," he said as he walked away with his buddies. "Next time, go play jump rope with the girls."

"Hey, stop right there, Eric!" a voice shouted. "I saw what happened here!"

It was our gym teacher, Mrs. Watson.

Eric stopped in his tracks.

"Eric, I saw you run toward Justin when he was running backward," she said. "I saw you push him hard from behind! Come with me. You and I are going to take a little walk to the principal's office."

"Are you okay, Justin?" Mrs. Watson asked. "Can you get to the nurse? I can walk with you, too."

"I'm okay," I whimpered. "I can get up."

I knew I had tears in my eyes, so I was glad to see Annie standing nearby.

"Annie, can you please walk Justin to the nurse's office?" Mrs. Watson asked.

Annie nodded and helped me to my feet. She picked up my glasses and guided me to the school building.

Here we go again.

"I saw everything after I pitched that ball, J.J.," Annie whispered.

"You didn't do anything wrong. Take some deep breaths. They will calm you down. In fact, let's do it together as we walk to the nurse."

We inhaled slowly and let out longer breaths. In and out, in and out. This was the same thing Annie did to help Ace calm down when he broke his ankle.

By the time we got the nurse's office, I felt much calmer.

"Hello, Justin," Miss Lolly said. "What happened to you?"

***

Later, when I got to class, everyone was in their seats. Bowing my head to hide my mangled glasses, I handed a note from Miss Lolly to Mrs. Lerner.

"Can you still wear your glasses?" she asked, looking at the tape that held them together.

"Yes, I'm fine," I said. "May I just go back to my desk?"

"As long as you feel well enough," she said.

"Okay, everyone, this afternoon, we will break into our groups," Mrs. Lerner said. "If you'd like to spend time on your art projects, you're welcome to do so, but please work quietly. I will be working with some students individually."

Ace, Brittney, Lexi, Annie, and I gathered at a table to discuss our art project presentation for tomorrow.

"Justin, you okay?" Annie asked.

"Yeah," I said. "Just a bloody nose. I put some ice on it. I'm good, really. Let's talk about our presentation."

"That Eric is a real jerk," Ace said.

Everyone nodded, and my friends fell silent.

To my relief, Lexi changed the subject.

"So I gathered some information during recess about which video game to choose," she said. "On the list, I had Spider-Man, Fortnite, and Minecraft. Fortnite won by a landslide! It seems that the guys *and* the girls like this video game the most."

"What can I say?" Ace said. "People clearly have no taste. Everyone knows Spider-Man is best. But, as a software developer, I have to go with what the people are telling us. Thank you for the research, Lexi."

We looked at him in amazement. Ace was taking his role very seriously.

Then Brittney said, "Sure, whatever our client wants, we will deliver."

Ace sat up taller and said in a deeper voice, "That's what I like to hear. So, what will all this cost me? Ya know, I'm not made of money. If the budget is too high, I'll have to find another team."

Ace laughed, and I grinned back at him.

"Hmm, I'll see what I can do, boss," Annie said.

We all started laughing, even Ace.

"No, seriously, Ace, you tell us your budget, and I'll let you know if we can work within it," Annie said with a confident smile.

"Justin's group in the back, quiet down or you will have to go back to your seats!" Mrs. Lerner called out.

I just shook my head in agreement and gave her a thumbs up.

I suggested, "We can use the sketch we created at Annie's house. I'll add some finishing touches this afternoon. Brittney, send me your type design, and I'll add it to my illustration. Then we can send all of it to Lexi, and she can create the PowerPoint."

"Okay, class, clean up and get ready to pack up," Mrs. Lerner announced.

On my way back to my seat, I asked Brittney if she wanted to walk home together.

She nodded yes. I acted cool about it, but inside I was jumping up and down.

{ CHAPTER 7 }

Heart Pounding, Head Pounding

Brittney met me outside the front doors of the school. My heart was beating so fast, I was sure she could hear it!

"Justin, how are you?" she asked. "Some kids said that kid Eric pushed you down while you were playing kickball. Is that true? Is that how you broke your glasses?"

"Uh, yeah, that's what happened," I said. "I'm okay.

"Hey, do you want to stop by my house today so we can sketch out ideas and work on the design and type?" I asked, trying to change the topic.

But Brit wouldn't let it go so easily.

"I'm glad you're okay, Jus," she said. "He bothered you at lunch the other day, too. You should talk to someone about it before you really get hurt."

I nodded but didn't say anything.

"Anyway, I can't come over today," she said, "but I'll work on the typeface and email it to you tonight."

I was touched Brittney cared about me. *Did she think I wasn't tough enough to handle Eric?*

"See you tomorrow at school, Jus," Brittney said as we reached her house.

I smiled and waved. I was a little disappointed Brittney couldn't come to my house, but happy we'd had a short time together that afternoon.

***

I walked into my house hesitantly. Mom would be waiting to hear about what happened today.

If the nurse called her when I went for ice, she'd know about my bloody nose!

My head pounded. I really didn't want my parents to make a fuss about Eric. It would only make it way worse for me with him!

"Hi, Jus. Please come into the kitchen," Mom insisted.

I walked in with my head down. "Sup, Mom?"

"What's up, Justin?" she said. "This is the second day you went to the nurse during lunch."

"I got knocked down on the playground," I said. "I'm okay."

"Your glasses are broken," she said. "I spoke to Dad after Miss Lolly called. He will be home a little earlier. Have a snack and do your homework. Then we can have a family discussion about what's been going on."

Without another word, I grabbed some chips and juice and went up to my room.

Upstairs, I noticed a bunch of texts on my computer. Kids from school were asking what happened at recess. I decided not to reply and started my homework. I needed a distraction, for sure.

After finishing the math word problems and social studies questions, I checked my email and saw one from Brittney. It was the completed logo!

I added it to the top of my illustration. Then I sent everything to the whole group to approve it and Lexi could add it to the PowerPoint.

As I hit send, an email came through from Ace. It had some pictures he'd taken of us working as a team. Our plan was to have Annie and Ace lead the presentation. It was all looking pretty cool.

When I was done, I headed to the garage to slam on my drums. Drumming always helped me with stress.

About a half hour later, Mom opened the garage door and told me Dad was home.

I walked into the kitchen, where Dad was sitting at the table. Standing, he gave me a hug.

He's not the sentimental type, and honestly, neither am I, but I sure needed that hug! As he held me, my eyes turned into waterfalls.

"I really don't want to discuss this, Dad," I said.

"How about you and I step out into the backyard and talk out there before dinner?" Dad said.

He gave Mom a look that said, *Dinner can wait.*

She nodded and said, "Try not to be too long."

Outside, Dad and I sat on the patio he had built brick by brick years ago. I loved sitting out there with him. It was our time to look out at the garden he created on his own. I was so proud of Dad for many reasons.

"So, Justin, I know there was another incident at school today," Dad said. "I had a phone call with the gym teacher, and she told me everything that occurred at lunch and recess in the last two days. Let's not get into the details right now. Instead, I'd like to tell you what your Jeje, my dad, did for me a long time ago when I was bullied by a kid named Charlie. Then we can see what our options are for dealing with Eric, so you do not feel uncomfortable."

"That sounds good to me," I said.
"Dad... how were you bullied?"

"Well, one time, he tried to push my head into the toilet," Dad said. "All of his friends stood there, laughing. I still remember, my heart was beating so fast, I thought it would pop out of my chest! Luckily, some kids came into the bathroom, and Charlie ran out."

"That's crazy, Dad!" I said. "Did you tell your teacher when you got back to class?"

"No, but I told your Jeje when I got home," he said. "He wanted me to learn some self-defense, so I could know how to handle bullies.

"After that, I took self-defense classes in my neighborhood. It gave me confidence, and even taught me how to avoid physical confrontation. I have found a place near here where you can take more up-to-date self-defense classes to teach you how to deal with bullies," Dad explained. "Would you be open to trying it?"

"It *does* sound better than having a discussion about it," I said.

"In the meantime," Dad continued, "I can tell you that Eric's parents were called by the school today. He will not be attending lunch or recess for a few days. The eyeglass store up the block is open later tonight, and Mom offered to take you to get the glasses fixed or replaced while I cook dinner. You can bring home some ice cream for dessert, too!"

"Yes!" I yelled, excited about the ice cream.

Well, that didn't go as badly as I expected.

I followed Dad back inside and wondered if I would like the self-defense class. *Would there be other kids my age there?*

My head began to pound again. New situations always made me a little nervous. But then, somehow, the thought of pistachio chocolate chip ice cream with all the toppings eased my mood and stomach. I had to admit, my parents were pretty cool.

***

After dessert, I went to bed. Mom came up to say good night.

"Jus, I know you had a challenging day," she said. "Try to get some rest. All of this with Eric should be over soon. We'll find a way, as a family and with your school, to support you. Dad and I respect how you feel about us not making a fuss. I hope you know you're not alone. We love you."

"Thanks, Mom. I love you, too," I said. "Good night."

Hmm, I wonder what she means by 'the way the school can support me.'

{ CHAPTER 8 }

Black Eye

I woke up thinking about the self-defense class I would be taking tonight. Dad said he'd come home in time to take me. Just Dad and me. I love that! It was going to be a terrific day because Eric would not be at recess, and my art team was going to show our project plan this morning. I knew we would ace it!

It felt good to look forward to going to school for a change. With a skip in my step, I made my way toward the line outside the school building.

"Hi Jus!" Brittney called out. I waved and went to join her.

But I also saw Ace hobble to the end of the line. He wasn't even looking for me. *Weird.*

Then I noticed he was wearing sunglasses and using a cane instead of crutches. I excused myself from Brittney and went over to him.

"Hi, Ace, what's up with the sunglasses?" I asked. "And why aren't you joining us up at the front of the line?"

"Um, all good here," he said. "Just a little run-in with my brother this morning."

Then he lifted his sunglasses a little.

He had a black eye! I wish I could say I was surprised, but I'd seen him with one about a year ago.

Ugh! I can't stand seeing Ace this way. I wonder if there is anything his parents can do to stop it!

I could tell Ace didn't want to talk about it, and I knew how that felt, so I just stood by him.

In the hallway, everyone waited for Mrs. Lerner. I wondered what she would say about Ace wearing sunglasses.

"Good morning, everyone," she said. "Please walk inside quietly and put away your personal items. As you know, we have art for the first period this morning. Uh, Aaron, take off the sunglasses when you go into the classroom."

Some kids giggled. Not me. Ace went straight to his desk with his head down. Mrs. Lerner called him over and talked to him quietly for a few minutes.

"Class, I will be right back," she said.

She and Ace walked out into the hall together. A few minutes later, Mrs. Lerner came back without Ace.

"Okay, everyone, please gather anything you need for art class and line up to head over there," she said.

Where's Ace? Will he be back in time to present our project? What if he's not there?

"Hey, Justin," Brittney whispered from behind me. "Where did Ace go? We need him."

I shrugged. If I had to guess, I'd say Ace was either at the nurse or the office, but I didn't think it was my place to tell Brittney.

Mrs. Randle met us inside the classroom.

"Please sit with your art teams this morning," she said. "We will need the whole class period for presentations. Now, who wants to present first?"

Many hands went up, but not ours. We all hoped Ace would show up soon!

"Is Ace okay?" Annie whispered to me. "Where did he go, Jus?"

I just shrugged again.

***

"Justin, is your group ready?" Mrs. Randle asked just as Ace entered the room.

He handed her a note. His sunglasses were gone. It was hard to see his black eye with the lights dimmed.

My group all looked at each other, confused.

"Thank you, Aaron," Mrs. Randle said. "Please, sit with your group. It is time to present your ideas. Are you all ready?"

"Yes, we are," Annie said.

Ace and Annie went up front to present, but we could all answer any questions.

Ace stood with Annie at our teacher's desk. With the lights off for our presentations, his black eye really wasn't very noticeable. Maybe the nurse had put something on it to disguise it.

"Annie, let's begin," Ace said.

"This first scene shows our team at Annie's house, where I told them the needs of my video game development company," Ace said. "We knew we wanted to advertise something you all like to play. I wanted an ad for a new Spider-Man game, but Lexi suggested I have her do a survey during recess to help determine which games are most popular. She asked everyone about Spider-Man, Minecraft, and Fortnite."

Annie showed some of the sketches and design layouts that we proposed before we knew which product we were going to advertise.

"Of course, Fortnite won," Ace said. "I have to do what the public requires, so I gave them the go-ahead after Annie presented the budget."

"Yeah, Fortnite!" everyone yelled out.

"Okay, okay, quiet down and let them continue," Mrs. Randle said.

"Thank you, Mrs. Randle," Ace said. "Now, as I was saying, I told Annie that I wasn't Mr. Moneypockets, and she came up with a reasonable budget based on the ad rates for Instagram and Twitter. Of course, this is all just pretend. I spent all my allowance last week."

Everyone laughed and clapped. Even Mrs. Randle giggled. She's a good sport.

"Thank you, everyone," she said. "When you have completed your projects, send the final files to me. You will be graded on the work and your group participation. However, this *is* an art class, so I would like each of you to sketch a small ad for the topic chosen by your group, which will be due in two weeks."

On the way back to class, Mrs. Lerner told me to go to the principal's office. She would catch me up with the work when I got back.

Great. What now?

***

"Hi, Justin," said Mrs. Bratchet, the secretary to Mr. Walker, the principal. With a warm smile, she said Mr. Walker was waiting for me.

I felt nervous and wondered whether I was in trouble. Mr. Walker met me at the door with a kind smile. He always had a way of making kids feel comfortable, even if we were in trouble.

"Justin, please, take a seat," he said, guiding me to a round table. This was where teachers sat in meetings. I felt like a grown-up.

"So, Justin, first off, you are not in trouble," Mr. Walker said. "I asked you to come here because the nurse and your parents have reported two incidents between you and Eric. I want you to know that he's suspended from lunch and recess for two days and will be in the office during those periods.

"Miss Lolly and Mrs. Lerner told me you did not want to talk about what happened, and your mom said you were afraid to make a big thing out of it," he continued. "I am here to tell you that all of this will be as confidential—you know, private—as you want. But please know, bullying is not acceptable in our school or really anywhere."

"I know, but sometimes kids get meaner if you tattle on them," I said. "I wanted to find a way to deal with it myself."

"Well," Mr. Walker said, "you are not the only one this has happened to in our school. Our district is committed to putting an end to bullying. But I need your help, Justin. I have carefully selected the first group of students to participate in an anti-bullying prevention team. To form this team, I have chosen some kids who were bullied, some who were bystanders, and some who were bullies. It is an honor to be selected, but deciding on whether to join is up to each student.

"Each student has been invited one at a time, just like I am inviting you. Everyone will have a choice to share their feelings and experiences. They will also help create ideas for this mission in our school. At first, some students you may not think you want to communicate within the group. But this is a safe and protected environment. Mrs. Pennick, our social worker, and I will supervise every meeting. I feel you could be an asset to this team, and we would be honored to have you join us. So what do you think?"

"Oh," I said, surprised. "I guess I can think about it. What would I have to do?"

"First, we will meet as a team with Mrs. Pennick and me," the principal said. "The plan is to understand this topic and strategies to help each of you individually. Then we want to find ways to enforce and share the strategies with the student body. Our first meeting will be tomorrow right after school. Would you like to just see what it's all about and let me know if you want to be part of this team?"

"I could check it out," I said politely. "Thanks for inviting me."

I knew my parents would want me to be respectful even if I wasn't sure about this anti-bullying team.

On my way back to class, I wondered what I would have to do at the team meeting. *Hmm… who else had he invited?*

***

My mom was driving Annie and Ace home today, so we all met in front of the school.

"Hey, J.J., why did you have to go to the office today?" Annie asked while we waited.

"Uh, all good," I said. "I wasn't in trouble. Mr. Walker just told me some stuff."

Ace was wearing his sunglasses again.

"Everything okay, Ace?" Annie said. "You did a great job in the presentation today. I'm glad you got to art class in time to join us."

"Yeah, didn't want to miss it," Ace said, getting into the car. "I'm good."

Ace seemed quiet on our trip to his house. I wondered what he was thinking.

When I got home, I took care of all my homework. I knew Dad was coming home early so we could have dinner and then go to my new self-defense class.

***

"Hey, Dad, can we get ice cream after the class?" I begged. I really wanted to have something to look forward to in case the class was boring.

"Sure, as long as it doesn't run too late," Dad said.

"How long is this class?"

"About forty-five minutes," he said.

I hesitantly walked into the building and quickly scanned the room. Someone met me at the door and asked me to take off my shoes. *I hope my feet don't smell.*

It was a large room, kinda like the gym we have at school. Kids sat cross-legged on the floor in organized lines facing a man in a white uniform and a black belt but no shoes standing in the front of the room. Everyone was quiet. To my surprise, Annie sat at the end of the first row. She motioned for me to sit behind her.

"Hey, I didn't know you were coming to this class," I whispered.

"Yeah, my Uncle Tom, my mother's brother, runs this program," she said. "I've been coming here for a year."

I suddenly felt more comfortable. I looked around the room. It was cool to see kids of mixed ages, genders, and cultural backgrounds.

Bowing to us, the teacher said, "Okay, boys and girls, my name is Master Tom. Please gather around me in a circle to welcome our new students."

Everyone bowed their heads back to him. I just copied what everyone did.

After the new students introduced themselves, he asked, "So who can tell our new students what this Taekwondo class is all about? How about you, Annie?"

"Well, first off," Annie said, "this class is a non-aggressive and honorable system of self-defense. Kids learn to defend themselves, but they also learn confidence and self-control. One example is if you are ever in a bullying situation. It's important to respond calmly and confidently before—and I emphasize BEFORE—it ever gets to physical bullying." She finished and bowed.

Everyone clapped. Annie smiled ear to ear, as always. I guess this is why Annie always seemed to handle being bullied with a chill attitude. She never yelled back or started fighting. *Maybe this class isn't going to be so bad after all.*

Then Master Tom told us to sit back in our straight lines.

Suddenly, the door to the room opened. I turned to see who was walking in. It was Ace!

What's he doing here? He never mentioned taking a self-defense class!

Master Tom turned, bowed, smiled, and said, "Welcome, late one. What is your name?"

A few of us giggled. Ace smiled, too.

"I'm Aaron," he mumbled. Then Ace saw me and winked. I couldn't believe he was in this class with me. This was definitely going to be a better class than I thought.

"Welcome, join our class," Tom said, bowing to Ace. "I will have an assistant bring a chair to the end of the first line so you may sit comfortably with that boot cast."

We all bowed with hands together, as if in prayer. Ace's face turned red. That just shows respect to someone.

"I am Tom, your *sha-bom*, which means teacher," he said to Ace. "Now, can someone tell us the main principles of our class only using words, not a sentence?"

A boy stood and said his name. Then he added, "martial art, Korea, self-esteem, non-aggressive, confidence, and self-defense."

"Perfect, *haksaeng*. That means 'a student' in Korean," Master Tom explained.

***

When class ended, Ace and I walked outside.

"Wow, I didn't know you were coming to this class," I said.

"The psychologist my parents see for Billy recommended it," Ace said. "I hope it helps me learn some strategies to deal with my brother while he's getting help for his bullying and anger issues.

"Listen, please don't tell any of the other kids about this," he said. "I think my mom spoke to your mom on Tuesday night, and she also suggested this class for me. I didn't want to come, so I didn't tell you about it. But after the situation this morning with Billy, I decided knowing how to take care of myself might be a good thing."

"I am so relieved that you and Annie are here," I said. "But especially you! I didn't know what to expect from the class."

Just then, our parents pulled up. We slapped each other five and left. I knew I needed this class, but I was even happier that Ace would get some help dealing with his brother. Funny how things happen sometimes.

On the way home, Dad asked me how I felt about the class and what I learned.

"It was pretty cool, Dad," I said. "I can see why you sent me. Today we worked on body language to prevent bullying. We learned that self-defense is not always about hitting back or striking another person. Instead, it's about checking our surroundings and listening to our guts, leaving before a problem starts, and using a confident voice. Then we practiced walking with good posture, which shows confidence, and we did some exercises to develop strength in our core and upper backs."

"Sounds like it was the right class for you, Justin," he said. "Do you think you want to stick with it?"

"Yep, and guess what the best part of tonight's class was…"

"Hmm, not sure," Dad said. "What was it?

"Ace and Annie were in it!"

"No, really?" he said.

He looked at me in the rear-view mirror and smiled. Something told me that none of this was an accident.

***

We stopped for ice cream on the way home. As we ate, I told Dad about the anti-bullying group.

"So, Dad, I had an invitation to join a special group with Mr. Walker and some others tomorrow after school," I said. We dug into the pistachio chocolate chip ice cream.

"I'm glad you mentioned it to me," Dad said. "Mr. Walker called your mom this morning and told her about the new bullying prevention team. Mom and I think it is worth checking out to see if you are interested. We have to give our permission if you choose to go. The decision is really up to you. However, it is an honor to be asked."

I took several more bites. When I finished, I said, "Well, I guess it couldn't hurt to try it once. After all, I was nervous about the self-defense class, but I enjoyed it."

At home, I washed up and went to bed. This day had been full of surprises—good and bad. *I wonder what tomorrow and that meeting will bring.*

{ CHAPTER 9 }

Transformation

When I woke up, the first thing I thought about was practicing standing with my shoulders back and holding my head a little higher. I tried it in front of my bedroom mirror. Next, I did some exercises we learned last night to strengthen our upper backs.

Looking in the mirror, I decided I needed more than a new posture. I needed a new look. Grabbing some gel, I played around with some hairstyles I saw other kids in my grade wearing.

I checked myself out. *Better. Much better.*

Then I remembered something Master Tom told us: "Walk tall with a sense of purpose and make eye contact with people around you to project an air of confidence."

"No dillydallying, please, Justin!" Mom called from downstairs. "Come down for breakfast."

Walking tall with my new look, I went downstairs.

Mom looked at my hair at breakfast, smiled slightly at me, and asked about last night's class. I showed her how I'd learned to walk more upright and with confidence. Then I reminded her of the meeting after school.

Mom nodded. "I hope you like the group," she said. "I'll pick you up when you're done."

On my way to Tara's house, I practiced walking taller.

"Hey, Jus, what's up?" she said. "I like the new hairstyle."

Lexi, standing beside her, added, "Yeah, something else about you looks different."

"Hey, thanks," I said, holding my shoulders back and looking each of them in the eyes.

"Are you both ready for the rehearsal at my house on Saturday?" I asked.

"Yes!" they both yelled out.

"Me too! I can't wait," I said. "I'll send a text tonight reminding everyone."

***

When I got to school, I saw that Eric was not back in line with the sixth graders.

Aaah, I can breathe. Another safe day!

"Hey, Jus, what's up? You look different today," Annie said. "Confident! Nice hairstyle, by the way."

I stood with my shoulders back and looked directly at her. "Thank you," I said.

Ace was in the line, too. "Hey, buddy, you look different today," he said. "New style. Cool."

***

During recess, I chose not to play kickball. Honestly, even without Eric on the field, I needed a day off from it. Instead, I just walked around, hoping to see Brittney. Today I was going to act more confident if I saw her.

She was standing near the cement barrels. She saw me first and waved.

I walked over. "What's up, Brittney?" I said.

"All good here, Jus."

She was holding a notebook.

"Why are you here all alone?" I asked.

"Sometimes, I come here to write in my journal," she said.

"What do you like to write about?" I asked.

"Oh, mostly poetry. Sometimes I write stories, or just about my feelings."

"That's cool," I said. "Sometimes I like to write my own lyrics for songs. We have a lot in common, huh?" I grinned at her.

"Yeah, seems like we do, Jus," she said, smiling right back at me.

"Hey, is it okay if I call you after school?" I said. "I have some really cool music to share with you."

"Sure, Jus."

I wondered if she could hear my heart pounding. I gave her my number so she could text me hers, and we agreed I would call around 5 p.m.

"Well, uh, good luck with the writing," I said.

Walking away, I felt like a prince. I was proud of myself for acting on my thoughts instead of worrying whether she would say yes to talking on the phone.

Recess sure felt better without Eric around. My head wasn't pounding, but now my heart was—for Brittney.

***

The bell rang and everyone headed for the school's front doors. Well, almost everyone. I started walking toward the office.

"Hey, Jus, where are you going?" Ace called out, walking in the same direction.

"Uh, I have a meeting in the office," I said.

"Me too," he said. "Is it with Mr. Walker?"

"Hey, guys, are you going to the meeting, too?" Annie called, rushing to catch up with us.

The three of us stopped. This coincidence, and the one last night, had us stumped.

We walked into the office.

"Come on in," Mr. Walker said, smiling. "Everyone will be here shortly. You all know Mrs. Pennick, our school social worker. She has visited many of our classrooms. We are honored to have her on this team."

We all smiled shyly.

"I'm happy and honored to be part of this team that Mr. Walker is creating," Mrs. Pennick said. Sometimes we call her Mrs. P.

"Come in, Ginny, Lexi, and Tara. Take any seat around the table," Mr. Walker called out.

Looking at the people Mr. Walker had chosen, I started to feel good about the group. Maybe it wouldn't be so bad.

Then Eric walked in. *Oh no.*

"First of all, I want to thank you all for joining us," Mr. Walker said. "You can see we have a good mix of students as part of our new anti-bullying team. We want your feedback to help reduce and even eliminate bullying on school grounds."

Eric glanced at me, and I looked directly back at him.

"The reason we have chosen the seven of you is that you've either been bullied, been a bully, or been a bystander," Mr. Walker said. "First, we need to identify what all of these terms mean, so we are handing out a booklet that provides information. You may write in it. The cover shows a picture of a poster we hope to hang in our school.

"Before we create a group mission statement, we need to clear the air about experiences we have had at our school regarding bullying," Mr. Walker continued. "I want you to know whatever is said in this room stays in this room. It is a pledge of honor. Can we all agree on this?"

We all nodded yes. I wasn't so sure about Eric being in this group, but I figured it couldn't hurt to listen and see what happens next.

"Okay, how about we start by sharing some of our experiences with being bullied?" Mr. Walker suggested.

"Well, I was bullied verbally for almost four years," Annie said. "It started in kindergarten and didn't really stop until the recent spring concert. No one hurt me physically, but I know what it is like to be called names, left out of social groups, and laughed at."

"Uh, yeah, that was me," Ace said, looking at Annie. "You know I'm sorry for bullying you. It wasn't until I got to know you that I realized I was a jerk. I have been bullied by my brother, verbally, and physically, so I really get how you must have felt. "

"Can you tell us about that, Aaron?" Mrs. Pennick asked.

"I'd rather not get into the details, but, at times, my brother verbally and physically bullies me just because he's older and thinks he can get away with it. Now my family is getting some help for my brother," Ace said. "Maybe I bullied others because I learned it from him."

"So Annie was verbally bullied," Mr. Walker said. "And Aaron is both verbally and physically bullied. Who else has had any experience with bullying?"

"Well, I often didn't say anything when I saw Aaron bullying Annie," Tara said. "I was afraid the other kids wouldn't like me if I stuck up for her. But when I got to know Annie better, I realized I needed to defend her when others were bullying or being extra mean.

"I even bullied her myself with Lexi in third grade," Tara continued. "You remember, Lexi, when we played that mean trick on Annie to get her to walk back and forth in the snowstorm?"

Tara looked sheepishly at Annie.

"Honestly, I started getting terrible stomach-aches after I remembered that," Tara said, "especially if I didn't speak up when someone was cruel to Annie."

"Not doing anything when you see someone bullied is called being a bystander," said Mrs. P.

I was surprised that Ace and Tara had shared so much. But they seemed at ease talking about it with Mrs. P. in the room.

Lexi was quiet at first and didn't look at Annie. Then she spoke up, too.

"Yeah, we definitely planned to be mean, so I guess that *was* bullying," Lexi said sadly. "I'm sorry, too, Annie."

Then she looked up at Annie and added, "It seemed funny at the time, but I'm sure it was hurtful. I hope you can forgive us."

"All good now," Annie said with a huge smile. She stood and walked over to them. She looked at each directly while slapping them five.

"Well, I know my parents want me to apologize to Justin," Eric said in a low tone.

"Okay, Eric, so what are you thinking?" said Mr. Walker.

"I have been mean to you, and I'm sorry," Eric said, looking past me.

I looked him straight in the eyes.

"Yes, that needs to end *today*," I said. "Thank you for your apology."

I was glad Eric apologized. Now perhaps I wouldn't have to worry anymore. Clearly, he had been a bully to me, but I wasn't going to say more. I was proud of my response to him. It felt good to speak to him with a firm and confident voice. I guess that class last night really helped me. *I just hope he really means this apology.*

"Were you being mean, rude, or bullying, Eric?" Mrs. P. asked Eric.

"I guess I was bullying him," Eric said softly, looking down.

"What's the difference?" asked Ginny.

"Being rude is butting in on a line or stepping on someone's foot by accident," Mrs. P. explained. "Being mean is doing something to hurt a person intentionally once, like calling someone a name or insulting someone about their appearance. Bullying is repeated mean or cruel behavior over time. Most often, bullying occurs when one person has more control over another in size or age. Really, none of these behaviors are appropriate, and they can all lead to more severe bullying if not addressed."

There was an awkward moment of silence. Mr. Walker looked around as we thought about Mrs. P's words.

"Great work, everyone," Mr. Walker said. "I hope this team meeting has been of help to you. It is only the beginning. We want you to understand what bullying is about. Next, we hope you will continue to share your own experiences and be part of this vital team in our school. Now, how did you feel about this meeting today?"

"I feel like this is a great team," Tara said. "I hope we can prevent others from being bullies or bystanders."

"I would like to be part of this team, too," Ace said. "But we need a name or a title, so it's official."

"How about we call ourselves the Better Than A Bully Brigade?" Annie suggested, with a big smile.

Most of us clapped, except for Eric.

Everyone in the room agreed to be part of this team, and we decided to meet next Monday after school.

I felt a little confused. It was good to clear the air with Eric, but did I want to be with him every time the team met? I wasn't so sure.

***

As soon as I got home, I ran up to my room, excited to call Brittney. But first, I decided to do some breathing as Annie taught me. I also needed to prepare some music to play during my call with Brittney. We always shared our art, but this would be different. I sat on my bed, took deep, long breaths, and slowly exhaled a few times. Then I did some exercises from the self-defense class to beef up my confidence.

Standing tall in front of the mirror in my room, I made the call. Somehow I was starting to see myself differently, even with my new glasses.

"Hello?"

"Hey Brit, it's me," I said.

"Hi, Jus," she said. "I'm excited to hear your music. What do you have?"

I played some of "Happy" and then "Count on Me" by Bruno Mars. I asked her which she liked the best. She said, "Count on Me."

"So, on Saturday, my band is meeting for the first time at my house," I said. "I can ask them if you can come to give us feedback. If they agree, do you want to join us?"

"Who's in your band?" she asked.

"It's a secret," I said. "We haven't told anyone about it yet. First, I have to find out if it's okay for you to join us. If the members are not ready for that this Saturday, maybe another time, okay?"

"Sure, Jus," she said. "I won't mention the band to anyone. Otherwise, you know it will be all around the school in minutes. Let me know if it's cool for me to come. Well, gotta go. See you tomorrow in class."

Ending the call, I felt a little dizzy.

Did I just do that? I called a girl and found plenty to talk about.

I was so proud of myself. I didn't freeze up at all during the whole conversation. Yeah, we mostly listened to music, but it sure felt good to share time with Brit. She's pretty and likes the same things as I do. What could be bad about all that?

Standing tall with my shoulders back in front of the full-length mirror, I saw a different me in the reflection—my new secret identity from the inside out.

{ CHAPTER 10 }

My Secret Powers

I bounced out of bed this morning! There was a new, lighter feeling inside of me.

It was the best night of sleep I'd had the whole school year. I quickly got down, did thirty push-ups, ten forearm planks, and twenty-five sit-ups. I'd learned how to do the exercises in Taekwondo. Master Tom said that keeping our bodies fit makes us feel better.

Not better. Terrific! Yeah, this will definitely be my new morning routine!

I also felt extra pumped because it was only one more day until our first band rehearsal. Everyone said they'd be there. Plus, everybody was cool with Brittney coming to listen. I think we all like Brittney because of her loyalty to friends and her kind personality—and because she can keep secrets. No one teased me about her, either. Of course, they don't know I really like her. At least, I don't think they do. *So what if they find out? Right? It's the new me!*

I ran downstairs, ate breakfast, kissed my mom, and headed outside to meet with Tara and Lexi. They were waiting outside Lexi's house with their bikes.

"Hey, Justin," Lexi said. "I'm really looking forward to our rehearsal tomorrow."

"Me too, Jus," Tara said.

"Hey, did you guys do the math homework last night?" she said, changing the subject. "The word problems were so complicated. I hate math!"

"Uh, it was so hard, but I worked through it," Lexi said.

"Oh no! I forgot to do it!" I said. "I'll be in trouble for sure."

"Well, you usually do your homework, so Mrs. Lerner will probably let it slide this time," Tara said.

"Yeah, we'll see," I said. But I wasn't so sure.

What if she calls on me to show my work?

***

"Everyone, settle down!" Mrs. Lerner said. "We will go over the math homework first period."

I opened my binder to a page with no answers on it. I guess I'd been too distracted by the call with Brittney and our plans with the band. It was a first for me. I hoped Mrs. Lerner would let it slide.

"Justin, could you please come up and show us how you did the first example?" Mrs. Lerner asked.

"Uh, I left it at home," I answered, quickly flipping my binder shut.

"Well, then, how about you come up to the front of the room and show us how you figured out the word problem anyway?" she said.

"Well, Mrs. Lerner. To be honest, I didn't get a chance to do it," I said.

Some kids giggled.

"Okay, Justin," she said. "Just use the five steps we learned this week to solve a math word problem. You can do that.

Reluctantly, I went up and read the problem out loud. Then I just stood there, at a loss for what to do. I looked at Annie in the back row. She smiled her magical smile, and I felt at ease.

Suddenly, a light bulb turned on in my head. I remembered all the steps we had learned to solve a word problem.

I'll just go step by step as we were taught. What's the worst that can happen? I'll just try my best.

I reread the problem again and followed the steps. We had been taught to show our work, so I explained each step as I went through it:

identifying keywords, circling important numbers, drawing a picture, writing an equation, and proving my answer. Mrs. Lerner smiled.

Whew! My voice didn't shake, and my heart didn't pound, even though I was afraid of being in trouble for not doing my homework. All this Taekwondo stuff seemed to be influencing me. I felt more confident in a difficult situation. Even if I got stuck, I knew I could just ask for help. No biggie!

***

"Justin, Aaron, Annie, Lexi, and Tara, please go to the office before recess," Mrs. Lerner announced as we headed for lunch.

Now what?

In the lunchroom, I headed over to Ace. In no time, we were all trading lunches as usual.

"Hey, Justin, why do you think we have to go to the office?" Lexi whispered as she munched on Ace's apple.

127

"I guess we'll find out when we get there," I said with a shrug.

"Hey, Lexi, look what I drew on my own lunch bag today," I said.

She smiled and took it from me. "Wow! That's a really cool picture of you playing the drums," she said. "What do the letters on the bass drum mean?"

Before I could answer, someone grabbed the bag. It went around the table until it got back to me, a bit crumpled but intact.

I smiled. The letters on the drum were BTABB.

"You'll have to guess!" I said with a laugh.

"I'll figure it out, Jus," Lexi said. "You know, I will."

I nodded. Lexi would definitely figure it out, but I wondered how long it would take.

***

"I hope this won't take up all of the recess!" Ace complained as he, Tara, Lexi, Annie, and I walked into the principal's office.

"Good afternoon, boys and girls," Mrs. Bratchet said. "Mr. Walker is waiting for all of you, so go right in."

Behind us, Eric and Ginny walked in, too.

"Okay, I will make this fast so you can go to recess," Mr. Walker said. "Your teachers will give you all a permission slip about our bullying prevention team. Think about a name for our group. I hope all of you will participate as part of our team, but I will understand if you don't. Our meetings will be twice a week for thirty minutes. Okay, go enjoy recess."

Walking out, I thought about the group. Mr. Walker always made us feel important and not just like little kids. He made us feel needed. It was hard to let him down when he needed help.

"Hey, let's head over to the barrels today," I suggested to Annie, Tara, Lexi, and Ace.

I hoped Brittney would be hanging out there, too.

As we walked, I spied Noah. I waved to him to join us, and he jogged over.

"So what's up, J.J.?" Ace asked when we got there.

"Well, I started a list of songs for us to practice tomorrow and wanted to see if everyone is okay with it," I said. "If you have other suggestions, let me know or text them when you get home. We will rehearse in the detached garage behind my house because my dad converted it into a music studio. It's a really cool space. I keep my drum kit in there, and Dad said we can use his amp for the lead guitar.

"Lexi, try to bring your amp for the bass," I said. "We have two microphones, so if anyone has an extra, bring it. My dad has a small sound system with several inputs for the mics."

"Wow, does your dad play and sing, too?" asked Noah.

"Yeah, he had a band a long time ago," I said. "We play together sometimes. He knows I will take extra good care of his equipment. He may pop his head in to see if we need any help."

"That all sounds cool to me," Annie said. "I'll make sure to bring music and words to the songs."

"I'll bring my percussion stuff, and I have an extra mic," Tara said.

"I can bring a mic, too," Noah said with a smile.

Everyone agreed to meet at my house at 2 p.m., and they ran off to play kickball. I looked around for Brit but didn't see her.

I wonder where she is. Will she show up at my rehearsal? Maybe I'll call her later.

***

On my way home from school, I saw Eric riding his bike, too. A little voice in my head told me to wave to him, so I did. Then I kept riding toward home.

"Hey there, Four Eyes. Where are you going?" I thought I heard Eric yell.

Oh no. Now what?

Suddenly, I caught sight of Brittney standing on her front stoop. I quickly pulled into her driveway.

"Hey, Brit. See you tomorrow, right?" I called, standing next to my bike and eyeing Eric passing by.

"Um, I'll ask my mom," she said. "If I can come, I'll be there a little later, like 2:30."

I hoped she'd come over and talk with me, but she stayed on her stoop. She didn't seem that excited about rehearsal.

Maybe she doesn't want to come, after all. Should I ask? No, I don't want to push. She seems a bit off today.

"Okay, maybe I'll call you later," I said with a smile.

Then, still a bit nervous, I headed for home.

As I turned the corner, I saw Eric. He pulled his bike up and blocked mine.

"Hey, glad we bumped into each other," I said without thinking.

Wait. What? What did I just say?

Eric smirked.

"Are you joining that team with Mr. Walker and Mrs. P.?" he asked.

"Yeah, I am," I said confidently. "And speaking of that, I don't like being called Four Eyes. How about knocking it off."

"Uh, it's just a joke, Justin," he said. "Don't be so sensitive. I told you I was sorry for what happened at school, and besides, we aren't in school now, are we? So I can't get suspended for just joking around. Really, take a chill pill."

I wasn't sure what to do. I'd acted confident, but Eric was still being mean. Then I thought about Annie and got a brainstorm!

"Hey, Eric, that is a cool BMX bike," I said. "Love the black-and-red detail. Want to race me? No one is in the street now."

"Uh, okay," he said with a smile. "Are you sure? I'm pretty fast, Justin."

I'm pretty fast, so why not? At least it will distract Eric from trying to bully me.

"Okay, let's line our front tires up," I said. "First one to get to the last house on the block wins. Let's count together. Ready?"

"One... two... three... GO!"

I quickly took the lead. I was lighter on my bike than Eric. I thought about losing, but three-quarters of the way, I changed my mind. *I can do this. I can win. I don't have to forfeit to get him to like me.*

"Wow, you are really fast, Justin!" he said as he caught up with me.

We raced two more times—we were having a fun time together! After I won another race, Eric took the next one. I think he respected my biking skills. The tension between us was drifting away with each race.

"Hey, maybe sometime we can set up an obstacle course in the parking lot by the school," Eric suggested.

"Great idea, let's do that!" I said.

Then he rode right up to me for a high five.

Instantly I thought of what Annie would do. To keep the mood light, I thought of a joke.

Hey, Eric... have you heard this one? What do you call **cheese** that's **not yours**?

Hmmm... I give up. What's it called?

Nacho cheese, man!

We both laughed hysterically.

"You know, Jus, you're not so bad after all," he said. "Hey, sometime could you show me how to draw like you do? I saw that mural you and Noah did out in the school hallway. It's really sharp."

"Thanks, Eric," I said with a smile. "Well, I gotta go now. It was nice bumping into you today."

"Yeah, we're good now, right?" he said.

"My dad always says, 'All's well that ends well,'" I said. "He has lots of those sayings. Yeah, we're good. See you at school."

I pulled away and headed home. I had to do my homework quickly. There was a free extra self-defense class tonight, and Dad promised to take me.

I hoped Eric's bullying episodes were over. It felt like we had a connection. Maybe I'd show him how to draw and trace characters from my superhero comics in the future. *Doing an obstacle course with our bikes—yeah, that's cool, too.*

***

Dad had to work late, so Mom dropped me off at Taekwondo. Afterward, she picked up Ace and me for the ride home.

"Hi, guys. How was class tonight?" Mom asked.

"It was cool," I said. "I found out earlier today I naturally used a Taekwondo strategy even before we learned it. Cool, huh?"

"What strategy?" Mom said.

"Well, when I was riding home today, Eric approached me," I said. "At first, I wanted to ditch him. Tonight we learned it is not a sign of weakness to run from a bully. In fact, it takes courage and strength. I did what's called 'keeping your eyes on the exit.'

"So as Eric rode over to me on his bike," I continued, "I saw a friend sitting on her stoop and I drove my bike right up her driveway. At first, I thought the strategy worked. But Eric waited for me and then blocked me with his bike. Right then, I thought of a different way to distract him. I remembered some of the ways Annie uses distraction to change a tense situation. I gave him a compliment about his bike and then challenged him to a race. You know I'm fast, Mom. In the end, we had fun, and he respected me for my skills."

Ace was listening, too. "That was smart, J.J.," he said. "I really liked learning in class how to physically block someone who is bullying you. Also, we learned how to remove someone's fingers from our wrists if they try to grab us, which was a pretty good trick."

"Mostly, we're learning to walk away before a situation gets worse," I said. "However, we're also doing exercises to strengthen our arms, core, and legs, and to stand up straight. We learned ways to develop a calm, confident manner for stressful situations. I really like the class, Mom."

After we dropped off Ace, I asked Mom if she knew he was going to be in my Taekwondo class.

"I spoke with his mom last week," Mom said. "She told me how Billy has been verbally and physically bullying Aaron. That made me think about what has been happening with Eric and you. I told her how your dad was bullied as a kid and where we were sending you to get some help while the school organizes an anti-bullying program."

"Yeah, Mom, Ace has had more than one black eye from Billy in the last two years," I said.

"So I heard," she said. "But they are now getting help for the family to deal with the situation. I wish we could do more, but what happens in their family is their business."

"I know, Mom," I said. "I'm just happy Ace is getting some help, too. He has bullied some kids verbally, but that's where it ended.

"Oh, that reminds me. I need you to sign a permission slip for me to be in the bullying prevention group," I said.

"What made you decide to join?" she asked.

"Some of my buddies are in the group," I said. "I thought about how I used to treat Annie. It was not cool. Also, Mom, you know that Tara and her mom have gotten our whole community together to help Annie and her mom fix their home. I think that is really kind of everyone. It will make it easier for her to do laundry upstairs, and it will be nicer for Annie, too.

"When I thought about what our community is doing, I realized that a school is like a community," I said. "It will be nice to participate in an activity that will help others make our school a 'no-bullying zone.' Just like you and Dad, I like to help people, too."

Mom parked the car and turned to me. Something about her smile told me she wasn't surprised I was joining the group. She had a sparkle in her eyes that said, *Now we're talking!* She put up her hand, and we high-fived.

"I'm proud of you, Justin," she said. "Now, are you all set for your band rehearsal tomorrow?"

"Yep, everyone is coming, and there may be a secret visitor," I said.

"Who is it?" Mom asked excitedly.

"I'm not sure the person is coming, so it's still a secret, Mom. Sorry."

"Just make sure you clean up the garage so there is room for everyone."

I nodded. Mom had a thing about keeping the house clean. I earned my allowance by vacuuming the downstairs of the house. Didn't love it, but money is money, right? And I already intended to make the garage spic and span, especially for my secret guest.

***

After dinner and cleaning up the garage, I wanted to call Brittney. She seemed a little cold when I pulled up at her house today.

Maybe she doesn't like me.

Then the confident mini-me spoke up.

Hey, just call. Find that self-assured voice. Be happy. If Brittney can't come or doesn't want to, you still have the rehearsal to enjoy.

So I called and asked where she was during recess.

It turned out that Brittney had needed to rest at the nurse's office. She confided that she was up late last night because her parents were fighting with her older sister.

I listened, but I didn't ask about coming to the rehearsal.

Luckily, she brought it up herself. She told me she would ask in the morning, when things chilled out at home.

When we got off our phones, I still had high hopes that she would come to the rehearsal.

Once you choose hope, anything is possible!

Yep, tomorrow is going to be the best day ever!

{ CHAPTER 11 }

One More Voice

I woke up to the sound of my cellphone ringing at 9 a.m. Tara's name was on my screen.

"Hey, Jus," she said. "We might be a few minutes late because I just found out from Annie that her mom has a job interview at 1:45 p.m. My mom is going to drive her there and then drop us off by you."

"Wow, where is Annie's mom going to work?" I asked.

"Their church has invited her to answer their phones and do some bookkeeping," Tara said. "But they want to meet with her first to talk about it."

My phone rang again. This time it was Ace.

"What's up, Ace?" I said.

"So my family has an appointment today at 11:30, and I have to go," he said. "I'm not sure I will get to the rehearsal by 2. It's all because of Billy. We are, like, in therapy with him. Sometimes he goes by himself, but this time it's like a family meeting."

Ugh. I hope this isn't the start of another issue for our band practice today.

"Uh, well," I said. "Just come whenever you can get here."

"Okay, J.J. Later," he said. Ace was not in a good mood.

I showered, dressed, ate breakfast, and finished cleaning the garage. Excitement about our rehearsal kept my mind busy, but it seemed like the morning went on forever.

***

My cell rang again at 1:45.

"Hi, Jus." It was Brittney. "Are you still having the rehearsal?"

"Sure am."

"Well, I can't get to you until 2:30 'cause of a bunch of stuff here at home," she said. "Do you still want me to come if I am late?"

It seemed like lateness was becoming contagious. *Is this rehearsal doomed? Still, late is better than not at all, right?*

"Uh, sure. Happy to have you join us whenever you can get here," I said. "Come to the back of the house. We'll be in the garage."

***

I raised the garage door at 2 p.m. and waited for everyone to show up. Tara, Annie, and Lexi arrived first. We started talking about which song to do. Then Noah rolled in with his guitar.

Yeah, Ace actually got here in time! His dad wheeled the keyboard into the garage.

I guess this is gonna be a great day, after all.

After everyone in the band arrived, we set up and tuned our instruments.

To get this jam going, I yelled out...

Okay, on four, now...
ONE, TWO, THREE, FOUR...!

Ace started playing **"Happy"** with a pulsating force.

"It might..."

Noah slammed it on guitar. Annie joined him at the mic.

Tara was dancing the **Woah** while tapping a tambourine.

Our sound exploded as we all sang the chorus.

Suddenly Brittney entered the garage, clapping along with the rest of us.

Instantly my garage became a sound cloud lift-off. The rest of the afternoon flew by in a musical dream. Until this moment, I hadn't realized how talented everyone was.

It doesn't get better than this!

Then my dad poked his head in.

"Okay, guys, your two hours are up," he said. "We don't want to disturb the neighbors. But you guys made fantastic music! You definitely have it going on. Please just clean up before you go."

Before he went back inside, everyone thanked him for letting us use the garage and his equipment. Dad was great that way. And he knew I'd want a little time without him watching us clean up.

"Okay, so what is the plan for our next rehearsal, 'cause next time I'll bring some snacks!" Lexi said.

"I'll ask if we can rehearse here again next week," I said.

"What song should we try next?" Annie said.

"Hey, how about 'Count On Me' by Bruno Mars?" Brittney suggested.

"Love that song," Lexi said.

"This is a perfect spot for practicing, and that is the perfect next song," Noah said.

"Do you think your parents will mind having us use the studio again?" Annie asked.

"No, 'cause we are out here, and they are in there," I said with a laugh.

Everyone else laughed, too.

"Hey, Brittney, thanks for joining us today," Tara said. "It was fun dancing with you."

"Yeah, you two have the moves," Noah said.

Tara and Brittney blushed.

"They do!" Ace agreed.

"It definitely added to the energy," Lexi said.

"Come next time, too, Brittney," I said. "It was terrific getting your feedback. Some of your pointers really tightened up the third verse."

"Okay, we are all cleaned up," Ace said. "My ride is out front, so keep us posted, J.J. See you all on Monday at school!"

My mom drove Annie home, and Tara walked home with Lexi.

"It was fun, Jus," Brit said. "Thanks for inviting me."

"Ah, want to sing a few lines with me by the mic before you go? I could tell you really like the song."

"Sure!" she said.

"I can play the instrumental on YouTube for 'Count on Me' using my phone, and we can sing along."

Smiling, Brit stepped up to the mic with me.

"Ready? One, two, three." I clicked on the music.

"If you…"
Yep, a rad day! Wow!

{ CHAPTER 12 }

BTABB

After school Monday, Ace, Tara, Lexi, Annie, and I walked to the office to meet with Mr. Walker and Mrs. Pennick.

"Hey, do you have the permission slip?" I asked Ace.

"Yep, my parents and therapist agreed with me. It would be good for me to join the group," he said.

Eric and Ginny followed us inside the office. Then Mr. Walker closed the door.

Mrs. Pennick was already at the round table.

"For right now, we are going to keep these meetings private," Mr. Walker said. "When we are ready to present your ideas to the school, we will reveal our team. We can add members, if needed, at another time. Please hand your permission slips to Mrs. Pennick."

"At this time, we are preparing for our next bullying prevention assembly for next fall," Mrs. Pennick said. "October is National Bullying Prevention Awareness Month, but we don't want to wait until then. Instead, we want to raise awareness about this issue now and maybe start a mural opposite the gym doors. One idea is to use paper bricks. Kids could write on them or decorate them in art class. Each brick could have a statement on how to prevent bullying. If you have any other ideas, let me know."

"What do you need us for?" Eric asked.

"You will all be part of an assembly kickoff," she said. "We also want your input on how to get everyone excited about the concepts. Also, you will be our eyes and ears in the hallways, playground, and on the lines outside the school."

"So, are we going to be tattletales?" I asked.

"I was called a tattletale for speaking up recently," I said, looking at Ginny. "It didn't feel good."

"Telling isn't tattling if it is done to help someone," Mrs. P. said. "When kids stick together and don't accept bullying, they can change these negative situations and the outcomes. As a team, you can make a difference for our school."

"Actually, you will be more like safety guards looking out for situations I might need to address," added Mr. Walker.

"Also, you will learn empowering words and actions to ward off bullying before it escalates," Mrs. P. said. "You wouldn't use physical force, but you would reach out to an adult immediately if you see trouble."

"So what did you think of my idea for the name of our team: *Better Than A Bully Brigade*?" Annie asked.

"Yeah, I like that one!" Lexi said. "We could use the initials BTABB on banners, T-shirts, pens, and stickers."

Lexi was always coming up with marketing ideas.

"Uh, Justin, is that what you drew on your lunch bag the other day?" she asked me.

"Yep," I said. "I liked Annie's idea during our first meeting, so I played around with it in a drawing."

"Anyone have any other ideas?" Mr. Walker asked. He always made sure everyone felt included.

"I really like Annie's suggestion," Ace said. "It sounds strong, like we are leaders enforcing anti-bullying." Then, Ace stood up and saluted. *Always with the drama. Gotta love him.*

We all voted to adopt the name.

"Okay, let's chat about what we could do for an assembly," said Mr. Walker.

"Well, what if we start it off with a concert by a local band? Kids love music!" Tara said.

"Do you know any bands that would play at our school?" Mr. Walker asked.

I looked at Ace, he looked at Lexi, and Lexi looked at Annie. We all nodded and smiled.

"Yep, there is one sitting right here at this table," I said. "It's mostly been a secret. This past Saturday, we had our first rehearsal."

"We have an amazing sound together," Lexi said. "Even Justin's dad loved it!"

"Can you be ready with a song or two for the end of May?" Mr. Walker asked.

I looked around the table, and those of us in the band all agreed.

"Please let me know the songs you would perform," Mrs. P. said. "If it goes well, we could repeat it next October during National Bullying Prevention Month."

"Well, I have a magic act I could prepare," Eric said.

"Wow, I love magic!" Ginny said.

"You could be my assistant," Eric told her. "I'll even teach you how to do a few tricks."

"Well, we do want everyone to participate with the team, so this could work," Mr. Walker said. "Each act would have to be just ten to fifteen minutes, so we have time to explain the purpose of the assembly. Does this sound okay with all of you?"

We were all very excited about our team name, a band concert, and the magic act. Somehow, this team of some who were bullied, some who were bystanders, and even bullies themselves had a new purpose—to help stop bullying at our school.

WHO KNEW MY BEING BULLIED WOULD END UP HELPING MY BAND GET A GIG?

"Anyone want to share how they are feeling now?" Mrs. P. asked.

It was silent for a few moments, but I could feel the mood was lighter than the last time we met.

"Uh, well, I sort of feel bad," Eric said. "I guess I was a bully because I wanted to hurt Justin. Also, I chased him on my bike after school yesterday. But, you know, he was pretty cool about it. It didn't even seem to bother him. I'm genuinely sorry, Justin. And I think we cleared the air, right?"

I looked straight at him and said, "We're good." I wanted him to know I was confident he would not be bullying me anymore.

"Well, I'm happy you have come to understand all of that on your own, Eric," Mrs. P. said. "Whether you are inside or outside of school, bullying is not acceptable and will not be tolerated."

"Yeah, it's not cool," Eric admitted. "I guess I liked the attention I got from my classmates when I bullied younger kids. I'd rather be racing bikes with Justin instead of bullying him."

"Good insight, Eric. I can see you will play an important role on our team," Mrs. P. said with a smile.

Then in a soft voice, Ginny spoke up. "I was bullied outside at someone's house last week," she said, her head down.

Boy, it sure took a while for Gin to share her story. Maybe where she got bullied wasn't at school. This is a tough one to share. You go, Ginny!

"Don't use any names, Ginny, but tell us, how did it make you feel?" Mrs. P. asked.

"Awful!" Ginny said, with tears welling up.

Her voice grew choppy with anger.

"Someone tricked me while playing a game and cut my hair with scissors!"

Mrs. P. paused. "Do you feel angry?" she asked, handing Gin a tissue.

Ginny nodded, looked at Mrs. P., and dabbed her eyes.

Ace, Tara, Annie, and I all looked at each other.

"We were sort of bystanders and didn't know what to do," Tara said. "It happened so quickly. Our eyes were closed during a game of 'Telephone' while whispering the words to each other, 'Let's play a trick on Ginny.' The person who cut Gin's hair ran into their house before we could say or do anything, except Justin.

"I just wanted to run away," Tara continued, tears in her eyes.

Ginny looked up in disbelief. After all, Ginny didn't know some of us were passing around a message, started by the game leader, about playing a trick on her. Nor did she know none of us were aware of what the game leader was planning to do.

"I am really sorry," Tara added. "I didn't know what she meant to do to you. I was stunned, at first. I didn't know it was going to be something so dangerous and cruel. I should have stopped right then, but I felt stuck and didn't want to ruin the game."

Looking at Ginny, Tara said, "Even though I didn't know what the person had in mind, just the words would have hurt your feelings."

"Yeah, it was frightening," Annie said, "and once the person ran into her house, Ginny ran off crying to her home. I didn't know what actually occurred because my eyes had been closed. So when Tara said, 'Let's get out of here,' I went with her. I'm sorry. I know what it is like to be bullied.

"Ginny, I am sorry this happened to you," Annie said. "What started out as an innocent game became a tragedy. I hope you will accept my apology and friendship."

Annie walked over to Ginny and said, "May I give you a hug?"

Ginny looked at Annie and stood. They hugged.

Ace smiled and spoke up.

"Well, Gin," he said, "even though I never got the 'Telephone' message, I am sorry this happened to you. However, I'll pass on hugging now," he said with a grin.

Everyone laughed. Even Ginny giggled.

"But seriously, I am sorry you were physically bullied that day," Ace said. "Anyone ever bothers you here at school, you let me know. If they bother you off school grounds, well, do what you did. Get an adult right away. Hey, you might like to join some of us in a self-defense class we take. I can give you a free pass. Maybe come this week. They have lots of girls in the class, too." He looked at Annie.

"Yeah, definitely try to come this week," Annie said.

The cloud over Ginny's head seemed to drift away.

"How do you feel now, Ginny?" Mrs. P. asked.

"I feel a bit better," she said softly. "Thank you all for your support. This was hard for me to share."

"Lexi, you haven't shared anything today," Mrs. P said. "Is there something you want to add before we end the meeting?"

"When I heard the message during the game, I knew it was meant for Ginny, but I didn't know the type of trick the game leader intended to do," Lexi said. When I heard Ginny's hair was cut, I called her up and told her I was sorry for being part of it. Now I realize I had been a bystander, and I feel awful."

Tara chimed in, "Why not share the brave action you took, Jus?"

"I ran over to the game leader's mom and told her what her daughter had done with the scissors," I said. When this person's mom called me a tattletale and yelled at me to mind my own business, I didn't tell anyone about it—not even my parents."

"Justin, you were brave to speak up," Mrs. P. said. "Some people will not like us when we do. They might be embarrassed to be called out or feel they have to lash back verbally. So what did you do?"

"I just walked away," I said. "My heart was pounding because of how the mom yelled at me. But inside, I felt good that the person didn't get away with the secret. It was horrible to see someone physically bullied. It feels good getting it off my chest here, though. What got me through all of it at the time was knowing I did the right thing."

"Thank you for speaking up for me that day, Justin," Ginny said. "If it wasn't for you telling her mom you saw what happened, she would think she could do it to someone else. This person is facing some consequences and came to my house to apologize. But honestly, I'm still pretty shaken up.

I feel better talking about it with all of you," Ginny said. "Justin, you helped heal my heart. Knowing I had a friend that day means a lot."

Ginny smiled. It was the first smile I'd seen from her at this table.

"Do we need a captain for our team?" I asked.

"What would a captain do for the team?" Mr. Walker said.

"A captain could help organize, coordinate, and get out messages to teammates," Annie suggested.

"Do you all agree we need to have such a person?" Mr. Walker said.

We all nodded yes.

"Okay, who would like to be a team leader?" Mr. Walker asked.

Annie's hand went up faster than lightning could strike.

We all agreed that she should be the captain.

"I will need a co-captain, in case I am busy," Annie said. "May I choose one?"

"Who do you have in mind?" Mrs. P. said. "We are a team, so we should take a vote on it."

"How about..." Annie started. She turned, looking at each of us. When she got to Ginny, she winked.

Everyone clapped. Leave it to Annie to make everyone feel included.

Yeah, being part of the Better Than A Bully Brigade topped off my week.

Maybe I'll have more friends and fewer secrets now... Feeling great!

Please leave a review on Amazon for
*Better Than A Bully: J.J.'s Friendships
& Secrets,* **if you loved this story**.

Your review will help parents and children
more readily find the book to inspire them.

SUGGESTED QUESTIONS
FOR EACH CHAPTER

Chapter 1 The Pickup

How did you feel during the incident with Ace's brother?

Chapter 2 The Intruder

Have you ever felt left out or jealous of someone? What did you do about it?

How did you feel about Annie's offer to Eric?

Chapter 3 Four Eyes

Why do you think Eric bullied Justin on the lunch line in front of the fifth graders?

Would you have told someone or just left the lunch line, as Justin did?

Chapter 4 Creative Relief

Would you tell your parents if someone bullied you? Why or why not?

Chapter 5 Hard to Believe

Have you seen someone physically bullied? What would you do?

Do you feel Justin should have told on Evie? Explain.

Chapter 6 Slammed

Why do you think Eric felt he could physically bully Justin again? How did you feel when you read that part?

Chapter 7 Heart Pounding, Head Pounding

Do you think Justin should tell his parents about the playground incident with Eric earlier in the story?

Chapter 8 Black Eye

How do you think the Taekwondo class will help Justin with being bullied?

Chapter 9 Transformation

How can you tell the Taekwondo class helped Justin's self-esteem?

Would you want to participate in this type of bullying prevention team? Why?

Chapter 10 My Secret Powers

Do you think this was a good title for this chapter? Explain.

Chapter 11 One More Voice

How do you know Justin has become more confident about himself?

Chapter 12 BTABB

What surprised you about this chapter?

Do you think it is easy to turn from being a bystander to an upstander? Explain.

RESOURCES

American Society for the Positive Care of Children

This national nonprofit organization provides a wealth of helpful information at americanspcc.org.

The society describes "The 3 B's of Bullying" this way:

1. Bully: 30 percent of youth admit to bullying.
2. Bullied: 1 in 3 students are bullied at school.
3. Bystander: 70 percent have witnessed bullying.

Centers for Disease Control and Prevention

The federal CDC website is a helpful place to start to understand the nature and causes of bullying and to address the problem. Enter "bullying" in the search box at cdc.gov.

The groundbreaking "Adverse Childhood Experiences" (ACEs) study produced by the CDC and Kaiser Permanente identified many childhood traumas. The ACEs list emerged from a 1995-97 study involving more than 17,000 people. Enter "Adverse Childhood Experiences" in the search box at cdc.gov.

Department of Health and Human Services

This federal agency collects and provides information from various government agencies on what bullying is, what cyberbullying is, who is at risk, and how you can prevent and respond to bullying. Go to stopbullying.gov.

Pacer's National Bullying Center

Visit pacer.org/bullying for resources, videos, and information on what parents should know. The center has a website specifically for children, and it publishes a newsletter.

"The Bully Action Guide: How to Help Your Child and Get Your School to Listen," a 2011 book by educator Dr. Edward F. Dragan

★ BETTER THAN A BULLY ★

J.J.'s Friendships & Secrets

BOOK #2

ABOUT THE AUTHOR

TINA LEVINE writes prose to inspire readers to be the best versions of themselves. As a classroom teacher and learning specialist for twenty-five years, she has observed children at school being bullied. These experiences, as well as personal ones inspired *Better Than A Bully: J.J.'s Friendships & Secrets*.

ABOUT THE ILLUSTRATOR

NED LEVINE, an award-winning artist, has worked in the publishing, advertising and art licensing fields. He was a special artist and designer for Newsday, a New York newspaper, for forty-six years. Ned joined forces with his wife to create illustrations for *Better Than A Bully: J.J.'s Friendships & Secrets*.

---

www.**readonbooks**.com